DRAW or DRAG

**Center Point
Large Print**

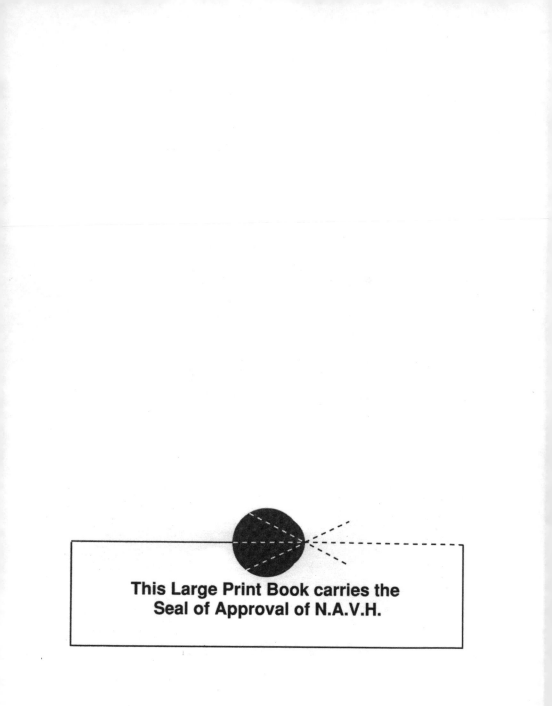

**This Large Print Book carries the
Seal of Approval of N.A.V.H.**

ॐ श्री गणेशाय नमः

WAYNE D. OVERHOLSER

DRAW or DRAG

CENTER POINT PUBLISHING
THORNDIKE, MAINE

This Center Point Large Print edition
is published in the year 2002 by arrangement with
Golden West Literary Agency.

The text of this Large Print edition is unabridged. In other
aspects, this book may vary from the original edition. Printed in
Thailand. Set in 16-point Times New Roman type by
Bill Coskrey and Gary Socquet.

ISBN 1-58547-227-1

Library of Congress Cataloging-in-Publication Data.

Overholser, Wayne D., 1906-
    Draw or drag / Wayne D. Overholser.--Center Point large print ed.
        p. cm.
    ISBN 1-58547-227-1 (lib. bdg. : alk. paper)
    1. Large type books. I. Title.

    PS3529.V33 D73 2002
    813'.54--dc21

                                                        2002022261

CHAPTER 1

THERE are men who play life as safe as it can be played, satisfied with their thirty a month and beans, satisfied to take orders, to have each twenty-four hours planned for them by someone else and to wind up their days riding the grub line or swamping out a saloon. But there are other men, gamblers born, who risk everything from their daily sweat to their lives for a chance to own their outfits, to live as free as the wind that daily touched the red sandstone cliffs rimming Long Tom Valley. And why? The reasons may be many. With Dan Reardon there was only one—the love he had for Sue Lane.

Reardon came down from the top of Garnet Mesa on a cold spring day when the scrub oak was beginning to show its leaves and the serviceberry bushes were faintly white with their promise of blossoms. There was grass on the lower levels, and within a week or so he could start his Rafter R herd out of the valley to summer range.

Perhaps spring had touched Dan Reardon. Or it might have been the prospect that he would have steers to sell in the fall to beef-hungry miners in the booming gold camps of the San Juan. Or the knowledge that this was the day he would be meeting Sue at dusk in the tamaracks along the Dolores River. Actually he was not conscious of any reason for feeling good. Without thought, he reined up halfway down the trail and let out an exultant whoop that ran in fading echoes down the steep slope. It was the way Dan Reardon felt.

The worst was behind him. He had a hunch it must be that way. A year ago he had quit his job with Broken Bell to start his Rafter R. No one else, not even Sue, knew it had been mostly a loan from his friend Collie Knapp that had bought his cow-and-calf herd and a few steers. Sue's father, Ash Lane, who owned Broken Bell, had not liked the idea of Reardon starting another ranch in the valley, but that was to be expected. Old Ash, bald and long-beaked as a great eagle, had his fingers on the pulse of Long Tom Valley. The little ranchers and the few settlers who lived there lasted only because Ash willed it so, a fact which they well knew.

It was Sue who had said, "Go ahead, Dan. I'll take care of Dad." So Reardon had gone ahead, buying the Nixon place at the foot of the south wall, clearing the sagebrush off the red soil, rebuilding the deserted log cabin and barn and pole corrals; for Reardon had known that the one weakness Ash Lane had was his daughter Sue.

A good year, a better year than Reardon had any right to expect. One more, and he could ask Sue to marry him. Now, with the echo of his squall dying among the sand-stone crags, Reardon looked out across Long Tom Valley, a forty-mile trough running east and west between high cliffs. Below him the Dolores River charged out of a narrow canyon, curled across the valley in a huge meander, and roared out through a gorge cut into the great north wall, growling and grinding its way steadily deeper before it reached the Colorado.

Westward along the Colorado-Utah line the La Sal mountains lifted their snowy peaks into the sky; eastward toward the head of the San Miguel River the San Juan range made a serrated line along the horizon. To the north far beyond the valley wall Reardon could see the Uncompahgre Plateau, spruce- and aspen-carpeted, deep with snow in winter but a garden of columbines and Mariposa lilies in summer, a paradise for stock with its grass belly-high on a cow. This was the land, an answer to a cowman's dream—summer range, a market to the east, and a valley where cattle could winter.

Reardon started down the trail again, some of his good feeling fading for no sound reason except that he was remembering Ash Lane's face when he told the old man he was quitting and had bought the Nixon place. Reardon had expected Ash to paw and bellow and get red in the face, but he hadn't expected the tightening of his lips under the bushy brown mustache, the frosty glint in the faded-blue eyes. Ash hadn't said much. Just, "All right, Dan. You've got a right to be a damned fool, but you'd do well to remember one thing. This is my valley."

He reached the bottom and reined his buckskin across the narrow bridge that spanned the chocolate-hued Dolores, hoofs striking with echoing sharpness upon the planks. The exuberance sputtered out and died. One more good year! Hell, he was fooling himself. He knew, when he stopped to think, that he had gone just about as far as he'd ever go. He'd have a ten-cow outfit all his life if he stayed here. Not that there wasn't room. Nor market. It was a question of pride with Ash Lane. *This is my valley!* When old Ash had said that, he'd said it all.

Reardon racked his buckskin in front of the Ripsaw store and stepped inside. There were a counter and shelves on one side; a rough pine bar on the other, and it was to the bar that Reardon turned. Jess Vance said, "Howdy, Dan," and came from the potbellied stove to stand across the bar from him.

"Whisky," Reardon said, unbuttoning his sheepskin coat.

Vance set a bottle and glass in front of Reardon, eyeing him a moment before he said, "It happened again last night."

Reardon took one drink and jingled a coin on the bar. He knew what Vance meant and he knew what was in Vance's mind. All the valley people except Reardon thought the same thing, and it always dropped a red veil of anger across his mind. That was the way it went in isolated countries like Long Tom Valley. Folks had nothing to do but it around all winter and think of things to say about each other. Mostly they dreamed up suspicions about Collie Knapp who lived alone on top of Easter Mesa, Collie who always had enough money to pay for his whisky and grub and had not done a day's work since he had come to the valley.

"How many?" Reardon asked.

"I'd guess a hundred. Pushing 'em like hell as always." Vance cleared his throat. "Maybe you saw the signal yesterday evening."

"I wasn't out in the valley yesterday where I could see it."

"I was," Vance said significantly. "It was just this side of Knapp's cabin."

"Ash know?"

"I reckon. He sent Link and his boys out to stop 'em, but, hell, a man can't guess where they'll cross the river.

No moon last night. This time they swam the horses over above the bridge."

Reardon stood turning his glass with blunt fingers, thinking of Collie Knapp, who had given him every cent he'd asked for when he had wanted a loan the year before. He burst out now: "Damn it, Jess. Collie ain't home much. He hunts or fishes most of the time. Just because some damned horse thief builds a signal fire up on the rim near his cabin is no reason Collie knew anything about it."

"Maybe not," Vance said. "Now get this straight, Dan. I like Collie. He buys a hell of a lot of liquor and grub from me, more'n one man could drink and eat in twenty years, and he pays cash. But what I think and how much I like Collie ain't got a damned thing to do with it."

That was true. The valley had condemned Collie Knapp from the first simply because he was different and because he lived alone. Sooner or later there would be a showdown, and Reardon had to decide how he stood. He knew, and he had known for a long time, what his choices would be. Either he would side his friend and fight Sue Lane's father, or he'd go back on Collie Knapp and help hang him. It was the devil's own choice. He and Collie had no chance at all if they fought Ash Lane. Chances were old Ash would wind up hanging Dan Reardon from the same cottonwood limb he strung Collie Knapp on.

Reardon's lips tightened. Loyalty had always been a strong compulsion in him. Even with the shadow of the loop as plain to see as the towering crests of the La Sals, he knew that when the finish came he'd be with Collie Knapp.

"Got an idea?" Reardon asked.

"Yeah. Tell Collie to get out of the country."

"He won't go, Jess. I've told him."

Vance shrugged his shoulders and looked out of a dirty window at the cottonwood tree in front of his store. "That's a good strong limb on the south side, Dan. It'll hold maybe three, four men."

If it would hold three or four men, it sure as hell would hold two. Reardon said, "Thanks, Jess. I'll go see Collie."

Reardon swung out of the store, buttoned his coat against the wind that seemed even colder than it had when he'd gone in, and, mounting, rode around the store and up the curling trail that led to Collie Knapp's cabin.

Knapp had been a mystery from the first. Perhaps that was the reason the valley folks distrusted him. He had come from a different world. He wore different clothes, he spoke a strange language, and he kept his past to himself.

"Got his nose in the clouds," they said. Or, "Too good to work and too good to have anything to do with common people." No, it wasn't really that way. Collie Knapp simply didn't understand the valley people any more than they understood him, so he stayed away from their dances. He never played poker at Vance's store. He was more likely to buy a bottle and do his drinking at home than to drink with the Broken Bell hands or the small ranchers.

It was midafternoon by the time Reardon rode over the rim. The mesa top stretched out before him, pierced by deep canyons breaking down to Deerhorn Creek on the south. Some of the mesa was covered with piñons and cedars, the higher stretches with scrub oak. At the crest of the cliff the trail ran between two close-set sandstone spires, an impregnable position from which one man with a Winchester could hold off an army. It had happened the only time a sheriff from the other side of the Uncompahgre Plateau had tried to catch up with a band of horses.

Reardon dismounted and spent ten minutes hunting among the boulders before he found the remains of the signal fire. Just a black spot ten feet from the rim. No tracks in the hard soil. A dozen cigarette butts. Collie Knapp didn't smoke cigarettes, a fact which would prove nothing to Ash Lane.

Mounting, Reardon rode on until he was out of the piñons and in the scrub oak. From here on anything could happen. Probably the horse thieves were sleeping somewhere on the mesa, their stolen herd held in a pocket or box canyon. They'd have a guard out, and the first notice of their presence would be the snap of a .30-30 slug. Or they might have slept through the morning and gone on, perhaps reaching the Utah line by now.

From the signs Reardon judged that Vance had guessed right. At least one hundred horses had gone through. Once beyond Long Tom Valley and in the rough country between here and the Utah line, the horse thieves were out of the law's reach. Or if a posse did have the temerity to follow and sighted them, it would be a bloody and probably impossible operation to capture them.

Reardon turned off the trail to Knapp's cabin. There were a few scattering pines here and a spring that had never been known to go dry. The cabin had been built years before by a prospector and deserted, and Collie Knapp had moved in without asking permission of anyone. He had brought a black saddler and a pack horse with him; he had built a small shed and a corral, and it had been all he wanted for a home.

There were two things that Reardon saw when he came into the clearing—a strange horse in the corral and a column of smoke from the chimney. In a way Reardon was sorry he'd caught Knapp at home. They had argued this time after time without agreement. "To hell with them," Knapp had said. "Perhaps there was a day when men were hanged on the frontier without proof, but that day's gone. This is America, Dan."

It was also Long Tom Valley, where the law was Ash Lane. That was the thing Collie Knapp could not understand. He would not understand it today, and Reardon admitted to himself with regret that he was wasting his time. He dismounted, covertly studying the horse. It was a roan gelding with a Star Y brand, a deep-chested animal that looked as if he had been ridden hard. Neither of Knapp's horses was in sight.

"Hello," Reardon called.

There was no answer. He stepped up to the cabin and knocked. Still no answer. He hesitated for a moment. Knapp wasn't around, or he'd have come out when Reardon called, but he had a feeling someone was inside. He stood motionless, listening. Then he pushed the door open and stepped in.

"Howdy, friend." A man waited beside the stove, a cocked gun in his hand. "You can stop right there."

A gust of warm air hit Reardon. He smelled frying bacon, heard its sizzle. Sunlight from the one window cut across the man's wide face. He wore a week's growth of red stubble; his green eyes probed Reardon like stabbing knife blades. He was short and stocky; his clothes were covered with dust. Reardon stood still, realizing that he was close to death. This fellow was on the run. He was tired and he was scared, almost panicky. It would take very little to make him pull the trigger.

Reardon remained motionless for what seemed like several minutes. Then the man said in a flat, dead tone, "If I was real sure you was a U.S. marshal, I'd plug you where you stand."

"I'm not," Reardon said.

"Then who are you?"

"Dan Reardon. I own Rafter R in the valley."

"What are you doing here?"

"I came up to see Collie."

"I thought Collie never had visitors."

"Just me."

Again there was silence, the green eyes still probing Reardon. Then he said in the same flat tone, "In my business, friend, you never take chances or you don't live long. Me, I've lived quite a spell and done right well. If I let you go and you tell what you know, I'd wind up dancing on air and looking at the sky. So I'd better kill you."

"I reckon you can do the chore," Reardon agreed, "but if I don't show up in the valley, there'll be some looking."

"I reckon," the man agreed.

"So you'd be smart to let it go," Reardon went on in a conversational tone. "Leastwise till Collie shows up."

"Now maybe that would be the way." The man motioned to come in. "Just don't make no fast moves."

"Somebody's coming now," Reardon said. "Collie,

probably."

Without taking his eyes from Reardon, the man lifted the frying-pan from the stove and set the coffeepot back. Then he said, "Turn around and walk out to the corral."

Reardon obeyed. Before he reached the corral Collie Knapp rode out of the scrub oak, leading his pack horse. Reardon called, "Tell your friend to put his iron up before he scares me to death."

For a moment Knapp seemed unable to find his voice. His handsome face showed bewilderment, then anger. "Put your gun up, Frisco," he said sharply. "This is the last man in Colorado you want to shoot."

"All right, Collie. I just wasn't taking no chances, but if that's the way you want it, that's the way it'll be." Wheeling, the man stalked back into the cabin.

Reardon burst out, "What kind of damned coyotes are you keeping, Collie?"

"I'm not keeping coyotes, Dan." Knapp grinned. "Did he give you a scare?"

"Scare? Hell, he was ready to plug me."

Knapp stepped down and stretched. He was taller, even, than Reardon and almost as darkly bronzed, a slender man with a boyish way that he had shown from the first day Reardon had seen him. "What brings you up here, Dan? I thought you'd be moving cattle."

"In a week or two." Reardon motioned toward the cabin. "Who is that hombre?"

"I've always known him as Frisco. Forget you saw him, will you?" Knapp rubbed his hands briskly on his corduroy coat. "Cold, isn't it? Reckon we'll ever have summer?"

"What's he doing here?"

"Forget it," Knapp said more sharply. "He won't be around long."

"You're in trouble, Collie," Reardon said. "Or maybe you didn't know a bunch of horses came through again last night."

Knapp's black brows lifted in surprise. "No, I didn't know, Dan. How would I?"

"They went by here, and a signal fire was built on the rim again."

Knapp shook his head. "Well, I can't help it if horse thieves use this trail. I've been down on the creek fishing."

"Vance figures you'd better move out, Collie. Old Ash is about ready to swing you. Me, too, I reckon."

Collie laughed as if it meant nothing. "They'll have a difficult time, Dan, but I don't want you to get into trouble on my account. Better quit coming up." He looked at the La Sals, his face suddenly tight with worry. "You've been a good friend, Dan, the only one I have. That's something I could never forgive myself for, getting you into trouble."

"How about yourself?"

"Me?" Knapp shrugged thin shoulders. "It doesn't make any difference. You're the only one under God's heaven who would miss me. Dan, sell out to Lane. Marry Sue and leave the country. Start again somewhere."

"Don't be such a damned fool," Reardon snapped. "You know I can't do that, but there's nothing holding you here."

"I like it. That's enough." He nodded. "I guess I'd better get inside and see how Frisco is making out. Host's duty, you know."

He stepped around Reardon and walked to the cabin in long, quick strides. Reardon watched him until he closed the door, anger building in him. It was the first time Collie Knapp had failed to invite him in for a meal or a drink.

⚜ CHAPTER 2 ⚜

THERE was no exuberance in Dan Reardon as he rode slowly back to the rim. He felt like a man trying to outrun an avalanche, all the time feeling the futility of his effort. He simply couldn't run fast enough to get clear.

For the first time since he had known Collie Knapp doubt of the man's honesty struck at him. There had never been any real evidence before, but the presence of this fellow Frisco would be all the evidence Ash Lane needed. Reardon had not budged Knapp. He had known how it would be, but it was an effort he had had to make.

Reardon rode slumped in the saddle, staring unseeingly ahead. He was caught in a web of circumstances which he had not woven. He wondered if Sue would understand. Even if she did, he could not expect her to come to him when the lines of battle were so clearly drawn between him and her father. It was the old question of loyalty again. She owed it to Ash Lane the same as he owed it to Collie Knapp.

As far as Dan Reardon was concerned, it meant nothing to him what Collie Knapp had been or where he had come from or why he was here in Long Tom Valley. There were plenty of men around, including Link Bellew,

Ash's foreman, who did mighty little talking about their past. Whatever the facts were now, there was one thing Reardon could not forget. When he had asked Knapp for a loan, Knapp had not demanded security. He had not set a date when the loan must be repaid. He had merely asked, "How much do you need, Dan?"

Reardon reached the rim and reined up at once, cursing softly. A dozen men were strung out on the trail below him, Ash Lane in front, Link Bellew behind him. Reardon pulled back so he would not be seen, knowing at once what he had to do, and knowing at the same time that his decision would be irrevocable.

Pulling his gun, Reardon waited in the narrow space between the two spires. Ash Lane appeared over the crest, then Link Bellew, and Reardon said, "That's as far as you're going today."

They reined up, Bellew signaling to the man behind him. For a moment neither Bellew nor Lane spoke. Lane sat his saddle like a great toad ready to hop. His blue eyes took on that frosty glint again, his lips flattened against his teeth under the bushy mustache. Breath stirred his shirt front; he started to speak, choked, and ended up with a bitter oath.

It was Link Bellew who would start trouble if there was any. Dan Reardon was not given to hating other men, but he hated Link Bellew with a deep and unforgiving passion, and he had long known Bellew felt the same way toward him.

There were several reasons for it. One was the fact that they both loved Sue, and Reardon had the inside track with her. Another, and this was the greater reason,

Reardon had worked under Bellew long enough to judge the man. He had seen him under circumstances that Ash Lane had not. He knew that Bellew was crafty, dishonest, and a killer, but he could not go to Ash and say, "Your foreman is a crook. If you knew what was good for you and Sue, you'd fire him."

Even if he did, Ash would not have believed him. He knew that both men had courted Sue, so he'd put it down to jealousy. But Bellew sensed that Reardon understood him, therefore he regarded Reardon as a dangerous man. Now satisfaction moved across his knife-edged face. It showed in his yellow eyes, in the small grin that curled his thin lips. Dan Reardon had played into his hands.

It was Ash Lane who found his voice first. He sucked in a long breath and shouted, "Dan, do you know what you're doing?"

"I know exactly what I'm doing," Reardon answered coolly. "You're aiming to hang Collie Knapp. I say there's no more proof now than there was the last time a bunch of horses went through here."

"Proof enough," Lane said in his loud, arrogant voice. "Since Knapp moved in here, this valley has been a highway for horse thieves. He's up here where he can watch the valley from one end to the other. That signal fire wasn't more'n a mile from his cabin. Now if he didn't set it, who in hell did?"

Reardon glanced at Bellew, wanting to say that it might be the foreman, but again he knew there was no use. "I don't know, Ash," Reardon admitted. "I hadn't heard about last night till I stopped at the store. Jess told me. I came on up and found where the fire had been. There was a bunch of cigarette stubs on the ground. You know Collie don't smoke nothing but a pipe."

"There's proof for you," Bellew murmured in his sly way.

Lane snorted. "Proof, hell. It don't prove nothing to me."

Reardon cuffed back his hat. "Ash, you've never been hit. Why don't you leave this business to the sheriff?"

Bellew laughed. "He says the sheriff, Ash."

But Lane didn't laugh. The frosty glint deepened in his eyes. "In the first place, the damned sheriff don't know we're in the county. In the second place, I'm going to get hit one of these times. I don't know who the outlaws are. Some of the Wild Bunch, I reckon. Anyhow, they know where to take stolen horses and where to get rid of them. So there'll come a time when they'll raid me, and I aim to stop 'em before they do. I've got some good horses I can't afford to lose."

"They won't ever touch you," Reardon said. "The Wild Bunch is a smart outfit. This valley is too important to them to take any chances on turning you against 'em."

"He seems to know what they'll do, Ash," Bellew murmured.

That was like Bellew. Reardon said, "Go easy on that talk, Link."

"I can add two and two and get four," Bellew pressed. "It's mighty funny that you're the only man in the valley who sticks up for Knapp. It's likewise funny that you had enough money to start out for yourself." He spat a brown turning ribbon into the dust of the trail. "A cowhand don't save that kind of dinero."

Reardon had guessed they'd think that, but no one had put it into words before. Lane stared at him, waiting for a denial, but Reardon didn't make it. He merely said, "I've seen you lose a chunk of money at poker in Gold Cup, Link. That looks mighty funny, too, don't it?"

"You try to make out that I'm in with these horse thieves?" Bellew demanded.

"You're in with 'em as much as I am. That's all I know." He swung his gaze to Lane. "The whole thing, Ash, is a question of law. Collie's got a right to a trial the same as the next man. Hanging him won't stop the horse stealing, but it will start something you can't stop."

"Maybe you've got a better idea?" Lane challenged.

Reardon nodded. "I have. Get the sheriff to send a deputy over here to watch the river. Have him watch Collie. If he gets any evidence, let him arrest Collie and take him to the county seat for trial."

Lane waved it away with a gesture of a big hand. "You're talking hogwash. I told you a year ago that this was my valley. It still is. I'll keep it that way."

"You don't have no right to hang a man," Reardon said stubbornly. "You're not God."

Fury was close to the exploding-point in Ash Lane. He stared at the gun in Reardon's hand, then lifted his eyes to Reardon's face. "You're holding the high ace right now, Dan. Next time it won't be that way. We'll get Knapp."

"If you do, I'll go after the sheriff," Reardon said coolly. "I'll go to the governor if I have to, and I'll have you arrested for murder. Now git back down the trail."

Lane didn't move. He sat chewing the tip of his mustache, Reardon's words bringing reason back into his mind. He said finally, "Dan, I pegged you for a smarter man than this. You know why I let you start your outfit?"

"Was it a proposition of letting me?" Reardon asked softly.

"You know damned well it was. For some reason Sue thinks she's in love with you, so I gave you your chances, but when you side a man like Collie Knapp, you're out of line too far. If you expect to marry Sue, you'll have to change your ways."

"I'll never change on this business, Ash. I've seen places where men thought they were bigger than the law. It never works."

Temper, long dammed up in Ash Lane, broke through then. He shouted in a raw, passionate voice, "All right, Dan. We're going back down the trail, but we'll get proof, and it looks to me like we'll be hanging you alongside Collie Knapp." He waved back toward the valley. "We picked up two Star Y horses below the bridge. We know they wouldn't stray across the plateau—"

"You said Star Y?" Reardon broke in. He was remembering the man Frisco in Collie Knapp's cabin. If Lane found the Star Y horse in Knapp's corral, this thing would be past the talking stage.

"Yeah, Star Y. Other side of the plateau. Belongs to a man named York." Some of the wild temper had gone out of Lane's face. "Dan, we're talking in circles and getting nowhere. I keep hoping I'll have a son-in-law I could get along with. Work with." Lane swallowed. "I hoped he'd be a man I could leave my property to and know he'd be worthy of it. I used to think you was that much man, but if you keep standing there with that iron in your fist protecting Collie Knapp, I'll know you ain't the man Sue claims you are."

This was it. You took a path because you had to, and you turned your back to what you wanted more than anything else in the world. It wasn't something you could reason out. There wasn't anybody you could go to and ask what to do. You only knew that you were no part of a man if you sold out a friend.

"You ain't hanging Collie," Reardon said.

"That your last word?" Lane demanded.

"That's it."

"Then you've got my last word. Don't ever come on my land to see Sue." Lane swallowed, a hand coming up to rub his face. He added, "Don't ever see Sue again." Reining around, he rode back down the trail, Bellew following.

Reardon nudged his horse forward until he could see the trail below him. He waited until he was sure Lane would not return. Then he swung around and took a fast pace back to Knapp's cabin.

The Star Y horse was gone. There was relief in Dan Reardon then. He pulled up in front of the cabin, calling, "Collie!"

Knapp came out, grinning in his boyish way. "Hello, Dan. Thought you'd gone."

Reardon said, "Ash Lane was just here to hang you."

Collie still grinned. "Lane is anathema to me. Forget him. Come in and have supper, Dan."

"I can't. Collie, them stolen horses belonged to Star Y. That Frisco gent was riding a Star Y horse. Where does that take you?"

Knapp shrugged. "Perhaps he stole one of them. I didn't ask. He's gone. Let's forget the whole thing."

"Collie," Reardon exploded, "can't you get it through your skull that Ash aims to hang you? I stopped him, but maybe I won't be around next time."

"Then they'll hang me," Knapp said mildly. "I've got a mess of trout—"

"Collie, I've never asked you why you're here or anything about what you used to be. I figgered it was your business, but this don't look right now. I've picked my side, and I'll play my string out, but I've got a right to know all of it."

Reardon had never seen Collie Knapp show strong feeling about anything. He did now. There was no boyishness about him, no hint of a smile in the corners of his mouth. His lips pulled into a thin line; his eyes were two black coals in a face turned white. He said, "It's still my business, Dan. I didn't ask you to pick my side."

"I've already picked it," Reardon flung back. "I want to know. Did I pick a horse thief's side?"

"No. I had nothing to do with that bunch of horses. I've never lighted a signal fire, and I don't know how Frisco got that roan gelding."

"That's good enough for me," Reardon said.

"About these trout—"

"No, thanks, Collie. I've got a date." Turning, Reardon rode out of the clearing.

✹ CHAPTER 3 ✹

THE sun was atop the La Sals as Reardon came over the rim. Shadows nested in the western end of the valley like incoming purple fog. Directly below him the bottom was bright red under the slanting sun rays that touched the long curl of the river and the Broken Bell buildings and the Ripsaw store. Then he was down, and the last of the sunlight died, and dusk was all around him.

Reardon hurried his horse's pace. Sue would be waiting for him, and Sue was not a patient woman. That was their one cause of contention. She had long argued that she wanted to help him build his outfit so that it could be hers as much as his, that a woman belonged with her man through the tough times as well as the easy, but Reardon had said no. He knew her too well.

Sue was used to having anything she wanted. Old Ash had given way to her girlish whims as long as Reardon had known them, but it was not something he could remind Sue of. So, without giving her his reason, he had clung doggedly to his decision that they'd wait two years in hopes he'd get his feet on the ground and some money in the bank. He wanted to build another room on the back of his cabin, he told her. Maybe he could even pipe water down from the spring.

Now, coming to the tamarack brush, he wasn't sure he had been right. He wasn't sure of anything. He was still trying to outrun the avalanche, and he still knew he couldn't do it. Maybe Collie Knapp had the right idea. Sell out and start over somewhere else. But he knew at once that he could not. Lane wouldn't give him a fair price, and no one else would buy if he had to buck Broken Bell. Besides, there was an inherent stubbornness in Reardon that wouldn't let him. He had never run from trouble; he wouldn't now.

Sue was waiting at the edge of the river. She called, "You're late, Dan."

He stepped down, and she came to him, lifting her lips for his kiss. He put his arms around her and waited a moment, looking down at her. In the thin light her hazel eyes seemed darker than they were, her chestnut hair that would be copper under the sun was almost black. A tenderness warmed him, a strange feeling after the threatening violence. His troubled thoughts turned to Ash Lane and what would happen to Sue if he married her. A man should not come between a girl and her father unless he could bring her more than he was taking from her, and he wondered if he could ever bring Sue that much.

"What is it, Dan?" she whispered.

He kissed her, and her arms tightened around his neck, and when he drew back, she laid a hand against his cheek. Then she brought her finger tips to his mouth, asking again, "What is it, Dan?"

He couldn't tell her. Not all of it. This was sweetness, good and compelling. She had never been long out of his thoughts from the first time he had kissed her more than a year ago; she had been the center of his life from that moment. Then his thoughts touched hard reality. If it had not been for Collie Knapp, he could not even have made his start. So he told her about Collie.

She listened, still and grave in his arms. When he was

done, she said, "Would you side Collie if you knew he was helping the horse thieves?"

She had cut straight to the core of his problem. It was the question he had been afraid to answer. He could not answer it now. He said stubbornly, "I don't know, but either way, Ash is wrong. He ain't looking for proof. He's already convicted Collie, which same even Ash Lane ain't got the right to do."

Sue moved away from him to the riverbank. She stood motionless, staring at the water, a black sweeping current in the dusk light, speaking with a liquid whisper that could not disguise the brutal force it held. Without turning, she said, "Dad came to the valley when I was a child. The Utes had been moved to Utah, but bands of them still came through here on their way to the southern reservation. I think they scared Mother to death. Anyhow, she didn't live long after we came. This was different than the San Luis Valley, no law except what Dad made. That's why he calls it his valley. Can you understand that, Dan?"

"Sure, but that was years ago, and Ash is still seeing the valley like it was then."

She said nothing. He came to her again and held her against him. She did not lift her face for another kiss. She turned so that she stood with her back to him, the back of her head against his chest, breathing hard. Hers was a strong, rounded body, and often when he kissed her he sensed how much she wanted him; he felt the shock of his own desires for her. He understood her impatience, but he could not forget that marriage was for life. He wanted his to start right.

It was different tonight. He felt the tension in her. He

knew that she wanted to say something but had not yet found the words, so he waited; and the last of the twilight ran out, and it was dark.

It might have been five minutes. Or ten. Then she said, "When two stubborn men set themselves against each other, it makes about as much sense as two bulls batting their skulls together. They don't reason. Maybe they get their horns knocked off. They paw and beller and raise some dust, but nothing good comes of it."

"What are you talking about?"

"You and Dad. I know you're doing what you think is right. So is Dad. He's never been able to see anything but his way. I didn't think you'd be like that."

"I'm not."

"You've told me a hundred times that you love me, but you say you don't want to get married until you can give your wife something. Did it ever occur to you that your love was enough?"

"No, it wouldn't be," he said grimly. "I've seen too many women who have lived like you'd have to. Old by the time they were thirty. One dress, maybe, that's good enough to wear to church and funerals. Breaking their backs toting water and living on boiled wheat. I'd shoot myself before I'd bring you down to that."

She took a long, sighing breath. "It wouldn't be that bad, Dan. You think I'm spoiled, that Dad buys me any-thing I ask for, but that isn't what makes happiness. He wants to run me. When I'm married, I'm supposed to live at home. Can't you see it isn't what I want, Dan? I've got to have a part in making my own home."

She didn't know. She couldn't. She had never lived like

that, but he had. He had seen his mother die before she was forty. The frontier was hell on horses and women, they said. The part about women was true, but how could he tell Sue so she would understand?

"Say it, Dan," she pleaded. "Say it and let me keep my pride."

"I love you," he said. "That's all I can say now."

"It isn't enough, Dan."

He told her about stopping her father and Link Bellew and their men on the rim. "You know how Ash is," he said. "He'll never forgive me. He'll do his damnedest to run me out of the valley, and if we get married, he'd never forgive you."

"I'd have you," she breathed. "My name would be Sue Reardon, not Lane."

"It'd be enough for six months. Or a year. Pretty soon you'd get to thinking how it had been. All the things you'd had when you'd been home. It wouldn't do."

"We've been meeting here so you wouldn't have trouble with Dad," she cried passionately. "We've been afraid to go to your place because somebody might see us, and there'd be talk. Is this any way to live?"

"No, but it's got to do for a while. I'll find a way."

"Do bulls that fight ever find a way, Dan?"

"We ain't bulls."

"You act like them. Dad's lived most of his life, but we're young. He'll never forgive and he'll never understand how I feel."

"I'll find a way," Reardon said, and knew he never could.

"Every day we wait we're cutting away part of our

lives. We can't reach into the past and pull these days back. Let's get married, Dan."

"We couldn't live here if we did."

Turning, she faced him and raised her hands to his shoulders. "Then sell out. Pay Collie Knapp what you owe him. We'll go somewhere else."

She pulled his lips down to hers. He could not argue with her. Life was a melody that had to be played right, or it had better not be played at all. This was just the first note. Her kisses could not carry him past that. Sweetness, long moment, holding her and wanting her and letting his lips tell her, and knowing that this was all he could take now.

Then she had drawn her head back, and he knew she thought she had convinced him. She breathed, "Here I am, Dan. Take me. I'd ask nothing of you but your love."

He was trembling and did not know why. She had debased her pride. She would never do it again. There was this moment when she was offering everything to him, and he knew he had again reached the dividing-point in the trail. If there was just this night, he could make his choice. But there would be other nights, and other days, hungry days, and he could not bear to see the regret that he knew would come to her.

Because he hesitated, she whispered, "We'll go to your cabin, Dan. It's cold out here. We don't care about scandal. Let the old women talk."

"No." The word came out of him in a single outburst of breath. The hungry days. Her red chapped hands. Broken fingernails. Pain from a throbbing back. The taunting triumph in Ash Lane's face. He said again, "No.

I love you too much."

She breathed, "Love!" and tore away from him. "You don't know what it means. If you love anybody, it's that outlaw Collie Knapp. You and your talk of loyalty."

"Sue."

He put out his arms to draw her back to him, but she would have none of it. She fought, striking at him, a palm cracking against the side of his face. She was crying in her anger. He had never heard her cry before. She ran toward her horse, stumbling and falling and regaining her feet. He heard her choking sobs. Then she was in the saddle and lashing her horse into a wild run through the tamarack brush. The sound of her going died, and he had never felt more alone in his life. There was the cry of a night bird, the steady beat of the river as it rolled past, and suddenly it was very cold.

❧ CHAPTER 4 ❧

REARDON saw the light in his windows when he was a long way off. He forced his mind to focus on it, wondering if it was Collie Knapp. Or was it Link Bellew and some of the Broken Bell hands? Perhaps Ash Lane had suspected where Sue had gone and had decided to give Reardon a lesson. A bitter grin touched his lips. He would welcome that. He needed a fight.

He pulled up outside the fringe of light, calling, "Hello."

The door burst open, and a woman cried, "Dan! Is that you, Dan?"

Astha Quinn! Reardon made no answer for a moment,

his mind running back two years to the night he had first met her in Gold Cup. She was a tall woman who stood boldly in the lamplight, her head held high. Her father crowded against her, staring into the darkness.

Reardon rode up to the cabin, saying, "It's me. I guess you're about the last people I expected to see."

Astha laughed. He remembered her laugh, as inviting as a clear stream rolling down a mountainside. "Surprise, Dan. We didn't find anybody at home, so we moved in. I've got supper ready."

That did surprise him. Astha lived with her father in the biggest brick house in Gold Cup. They had a Chinese cook and a woman to keep house, and Reardon had always thought that Astha did nothing but wear a different dress each day and entertain. He said, "I'll be in as soon as I put my horse up."

Pat Quinn stepped past Astha and walked to the watering-trough beside Reardon's horse. "I guess we shouldn't have come in on you this way, Dan, but I didn't know I was going to be able to get away right now. When the chance came, we just pulled out."

"Glad you did," Reardon said.

He stepped down and let his horse drink, wondering about this. Pat Quinn was the biggest man in Gold Cup. He owned the American Girl mine, the bank, and several of the businesses. He was an aggressive, raw-boned Irishman, red of face, with a booming laugh and an air of friendliness. Years ago he had made the strike that had given Gold Cup its birth, and he had been shrewd enough to capitalize on every opportunity that had come his way.

Reardon had met the Quinns two years before when he

had helped drive Lane's herd to the mining camp. It was Quinn's habit to invite the crew into his home for supper and some cards afterward, but this time Astha had taken a look at Dan and said no cards. There was a dance in the Odd Fellows' Hall, and they were going. So they had gone, Pat Quinn along with the rest. In a way it was a key to the relationship between Astha and her father. Even in business matters, she was likely to overrule him and have her way.

Now Quinn cleared his throat. As Reardon pulled the saddle off, Quinn said, "Remember at Placerville last winter I told you I was aiming to go into the cattle business?"

"I remember," Reardon said.

He had gone to Placerville to catch the train to Montrose and had run into Quinn, who was on his way to Denver. At the time Quinn had hinted he'd have a job for Reardon, and Reardon had said flatly he wouldn't be interested, he was in business for himself. Now he wondered if Quinn had driven all the way to Long Tom Valley to try to get him to change his mind.

Quinn waited until the buckskin was in the corral. He swung into step with Reardon as they walked to the cabin, Quinn saying, "I've been thinking of a deal that will make me a richer man than I am, and I'm here to let you in on it. As a matter of fact, Astha insisted that I give you the chance. Understand that I wasn't against you." He cleared his throat again. "But it was Astha's idea. She likes you." He laughed. "I guess you knew that."

Uneasiness began working in Reardon. He knew, all right. Astha Quinn was not a woman to hide her affections. She had written to him after he'd come back to the valley, and he'd answered. After that the letters had gone back and forth steadily and often until a year ago. He had liked Astha and he still did. It was just a case of loving Sue.

They went into the house, Reardon leaving the door open because Astha had a tremendous fire going. She was taking biscuits from the oven when her father and Reardon came in. Grimacing, she set the pan on the back of the stove.

"I don't mind saying, Dan, that you must have the worst stove in Long Tom Valley. First it wouldn't draw and now it practically burns my biscuits up."

Reardon grinned. "That stove's just like a woman."

Astha lifted the biscuits from the pan to a plate. "What do you mean by that?"

"Never the same twice."

She straightened, one hand coming up to press a curl of black hair into place. "Maybe some women are like that. I'm not."

"Oh, he didn't mean you," Quinn cut in.

Astha walked to the table and set the plate of biscuits in the center. She turned, dark eyes on Reardon. "Well, I don't know. You'd better be good to me to make up for that remark, mister."

He didn't feel like joshing her. He let it go with, "I'll be good to you, the rest of my life."

That was the wrong thing to say. He saw it as soon as Astha smiled. It was a special smile, the kind a woman reserved for a particular man. There had been rare moments when he had been alone with Sue that she had let her smile tell him she loved him. Now he saw, with a sudden pang of fear, that same fleeting tenderness on Astha's face he had seen on Sue's.

"I'll forgive you if you'll keep that promise. How about pouring the coffee, Dan? I think the potatoes are done."

It was a good meal, a better meal than Reardon ever cooked for himself. Once Quinn started to say, "It's a funny thing, I guess, but common enough for a man to spread out into other businesses than the one he knows. Now I've had an ambition to go into the cattle—"

"Dad!" Astha said sharply. "You promised you wouldn't talk business until after supper."

"Sorry." Quinn winked at Reardon. "She's hell on promises, Dan."

"I suppose Dad hasn't offered our apologies," Astha said, "for coming in on you this way. It's unforgivable, but we asked at the store and we were told there wasn't a hotel in the valley."

"There ain't," Reardon said. "You're welcome to stay here, of course, but after the kind of house—"

Astha shook her head at him. "Let's have no more of that. Dan, you don't know how I hate that monstrous castle Dad built. I'd have more than one room, but I certainly wouldn't have fifteen."

"Oh, hell," Quinn groaned. "If you think I'm going to sell—"

"Then keep it," Astha said tartly. "And I don't mind saying, Dan, that a bedroom on the back of this cabin would make it my ideal of a place to live."

"With a new stove," Reardon added.

There was a dimple in Astha's right cheek when she smiled. "Get me a new stove for a wedding present, Dan."

Reardon lowered his eyes and helped himself to a second piece of dried-apple pie. He didn't like the way the talk was going.

"Don't worry about accommodations, Dan," Quinn said.

"Astha can have the bunk." Reardon motioned toward it. "You and me can make out in the barn."

"No you won't," she cut in. "You can make your beds on the floor. I'd be afraid to stay here by myself."

Reardon stabbed at his pie, wondering what Sue would say if she heard about this.

Quinn scooted back his chair and patted his stomach. "Damned good meal, daughter. Guess I'll fire the cook."

"Better think twice, Dad," Astha said lightly. "I'll cook for Dan, but not for you."

"Now can we talk business?" Quinn demanded, lifting cigars from his pocket and offering one to Reardon.

Astha rose. "Of course. I'll do the dishes."

Quinn bit off the end of his cigar and lighted it. "Dan, you know how it is in Gold Cup. I'm the daddy of the town, and it's always graveled me to see Ash Lane drive a herd up there every fall and make a big profit selling to our butchers. So I'm going to do something about it. I'm going to buy all the land I can get in Long Tom Valley and have my own ranch. I might just as well have part of that profit as Lane."

"You're barking up the wrong tree," Reardon said. "This is Lane's valley."

"Yeah, I know." Quinn canted his chair back against

the wall and blew out a long plume of smoke. "That is, I know Lane makes his brag, but I'll bust him. I'll bust any man who stands in my way, and I've made up my mind. Now, I need you. I admit I don't know a good steer when I see one. I'll likewise admit I'm selfish in making this offer because I figger you're the one man I can trust." He motioned to Astha. "She says that, too."

"It won't work, Pat. The minute you try it, you'll have a range war on your hands."

"Okay," Quinn said. "We'll have a range war if Lane wants it, but I'll win. All I want you to do is to handle the cattle. I'll see that you have the gun hands you need to beat Ash Lane's ears off his head. I won't do a damned thing to start the war, but if he starts it, I'll finish it."

"I say it won't work," Reardon said doggedly. "In the first place, there ain't much patented land in the valley."

Quinn took the cigar out of his mouth, red face mirroring puzzlement. "Well, now, I hadn't thought of that. Who does own this land?"

"Uncle Sam."

"But there must be a dozen families in the valley besides Lane."

Reardon nodded, looking down at the cigar Quinn had given him. "That's right, but they're hooked up with Ash. Some of them are nesters who have proved up on their homesteads. They raise all the hay and grain Ash can use, and there's a sort of verbal agreement between 'em that he won't bother 'em as long as they deal with him."

Quinn put the cigar back into his mouth and chewed on it for a moment. Then he asked, "Ain't there some other ranches?"

"Ten-cow outfits about like mine. The idea is that they share the range with Broken Bell as long as they keep their herds down. Then at roundup time they work for Broken Bell. That way Ash gets by with less men than he'd otherwise need."

"Well then," Quinn said, "I'll buy those boys out. Maybe some of the settlers to boot."

Reardon fished a match out of his vest pocket and lighted his cigar. "Pat, I worked for Broken Bell for two years and I've had this outfit for one. In that time you get to know every man in a valley like this, the size hat he wears, what he eats, and what he thinks. I know what I'm talking about. You couldn't touch any of them."

Quinn showed his doubt. "Now, now, Dan. I don't know these fellows, but I know what money will do."

"Go ahead. Try it. You're too good a businessman to pay ten prices, and that's what it would take."

"Why?"

"Most of 'em are afraid of Ash. That's part of the answer. The rest of it is that they've got what they want. A living. Protection. A law that favors them as long as they play Ash's game."

"What kind of law?" Quinn asked sardonically.

"Ash Lane's law."

"How come you're here? Do you play along with Lane?"

Reardon took the cigar out of his mouth and glowered at it. "No. That's the reason you don't want me in this business. If he didn't fight you on account of you moving into the valley, he sure as hell would to get at me."

Astha turned from the stove where she was washing

dishes. "Dan, how did Ash happen to let you start up your own outfit?"

She stood with the lamplight full upon her strong, shapely body. Suddenly bitterness was in Reardon. If Sue could be a little more like Astha! There had never been any argument between him and Astha. She had always been easygoing, willing to go more than halfway, with none of the impatience that was so much a part of Sue.

Reardon lowered his eyes. "I was—engaged to Sue. I guess she held Ash off."

"I see," Astha said, and turned back to her dishpan.

Quinn cleared his throat noisily. "Now look, Dan. I ain't giving this notion up."

"There's other valleys," Reardon said.

"I want this one. Two reasons. It's perfect for wintering stock. Second reason is I aim to bust Lane. I've got to. He's had the Gold Cup market sewed up for years. I've lined up most of the butchers, but there's a few rebels, so I've got to work on it at both ends."

"You'll never bust Ash. He's got too much money."

"Money," Quinn snorted. "That's where you're wrong, Dan. He banks with me. I know exactly how he stands. He's the same as a lot of stockmen. Long on cattle but damned short on cash. As a matter of fact, he owes me more than he'd ever admit."

Pat Quinn was honest in stating his intentions. Now, meeting Quinn's eyes, Reardon was aware for the first time how ruthless the man was. Once he had set out to accomplish something, he would continue on that line regardless of the misery he brought to those in his way.

"I didn't know that," Dan said.

Quinn motioned with a big hand. "Not many do, and I don't go around talking about other men's business, but I trust you. Now I've got one question. Why is Ash down on you? Did you bust up with his girl?"

"No." Reardon took the cigar from his mouth and told Quinn about Collie Knapp. "It's been coming, Pat. Now it's here. Maybe I'm the damnedest fool in the valley, but I can't sit around and let him hang a man who's been a good friend of mine."

Quinn rose. "You're right, Dan. You were never more right in anything in your life. Folks have called me a lot of things, but whatever I have set out to do, I have never gone against the law." He waggled a thick finger at Reardon. "What you've just told me proves what I've always felt about you. Astha's said the same. Come hell or high water, you'll stick to what you think is right."

"Don't count me in on your scheme, Pat," Reardon warned. "I'll fight it out myself."

"You'll be licked if you try it alone. With me you'll win." Quinn walked to the stove and dropped his cigar butt into it. "I tell you I'm going ahead. We'll start with your quarter section. I'll buy other land if and when I can, but this will do for a beginning, and I aim to tell Lane what he's in for." He grinned. "If I judge you right, Dan, you ain't afraid of a fight."

"I ain't afraid of a fight." Reardon rose and moved toward the table. "I just don't want any part of this."

❧ CHAPTER 5 ❧

QUINN stood spread-legged, anger darkening his face. Astha had taken off her apron. Now she turned from hanging up the dishcloth back of the stove, saying brightly, "Let's take a walk, Dan. It's still winter in Gold Cup. This seems like the tropics."

"It's cold," Dan said.

Quinn yawned. "Well, I'm going to bed." He took off his coat. "Here, Astha."

"I'm not going to bundle up like that." Astha reached for her coat. "I won't need anything besides this."

"I'll sleep in the barn." Reardon motioned to a box in the corner. "There's a blanket over there. Hope the floor won't be too hard."

"I've slept on harder boards than you've got." Quinn yawned again. "There's a robe in the buggy. I'll get it."

Astha had moved to the door. "Coming, Dan?"

He reached for his sheepskin and slid into it. Conscience stirred in him, for he was thinking again of Sue. He was remembering her anger tonight, remembering that she had slapped him, and the stirring of his conscience died under the sudden rush of resentment. Sue was still wearing his ring, but it was probably because she had forgotten to take it off.

"Sure, I'm coming," Reardon said.

Astha took his arm when they were through the door. They moved slowly toward the county road, Astha's head thrown back, her eyes on the sky. She said softly, "It's like black velvet set with diamonds. You know, Dan, I'm awfully tired of the ten months of winter we have in Gold Cup. It feels and smells like spring down here." She sighed. "I envy you."

He held his silence, surprised by a sense of closeness that was upon them. He had forgotten how much he had been drawn to her when he had been with her in Gold Cup. She was a strong, vibrant woman, yet there was always a tenderness in her, an unspoken understanding.

They walked a dozen steps before she asked, "You're still engaged to Sue?"

"I don't know," he said miserably.

Again the silence ran out for another dozen steps. Then she said, "I don't mean to pry and I know it's none of my business, but is it because of her father?"

"Partly. And Collie Knapp."

"I guess," she murmured, "that women look at these things differently, but it seems to me that if a woman loves a man, even her own father could not be between them."

"It's more than that," he said. "She wants to get married now. Trouble is I've never had anything, and right now I don't see much chance of getting ahead."

She stopped and faced him. The light was too thin to see her expression, but he sensed the feeling that was in her. She asked, "Dan, how old are you?"

"Twenty-five."

"Funny," she said softly. "You've changed. Two years ago you seemed younger than twenty-three. Now you seem older than twenty-five."

No, it wasn't funny. Not to a man who had lived through this last year; its hopes and its fears, the wild clawing for something better than he had ever known.

Now he realized he couldn't expect it. He would be a dead man if he stayed, a beaten man if he ran.

"Tonight I'm a hundred years old," he said.

"You'll never be that old, Dan. What do you want from life?"

He wanted Sue and a decent living, a chance to work for her and give her the kind of home she was used to, the security a man should have if he was to raise a family, but he couldn't say that to Astha Quinn. So he said, "My own life, I guess. I don't want to be beholden to anyone."

"You can have your own life if you take Dad's offer."

"I'll make my own way—"

"Now you're talking crazy. It was a fair deal, your cow savvy for his money. You'd both profit."

He said without thinking, "I got the idea you went with the deal."

She flinched and drew back, and he wished he could unsay the words. He said quickly, "I'm sorry. I didn't mean it that way. I've had my sights set on one thing, and it's hard to change."

"I know. I guess we'd better go back."

They turned and walked to the house, and shame was in him. Whatever selfish motives might have been in Pat Quinn were not in Astha. He had seen her tonight in a different light than he had ever pictured her before. She was used to luxuries that even Sue had not known, but she was not above battling a stubborn stove and cooking a meal and putting her hands in dishwater.

They reached the house and stopped in the shaft of light from the window. She breathed, "I'll go in now. I'm sorry about taking your bed."

He put his hands on her shoulders and looked at her for a long moment, wondering if he had set his sights on the wrong thing. Her eyes were dark brown, possessed of a gentleness he had not seen two years ago. Her hair, as black as the great wall behind him, was softly curled above her forehead. There was a small smile in the corners of her lips, lips that were full and red and expressive, and he sensed there were words locked behind them she wanted to say and could not.

"I'm sorry I said that," he told her. "Seemed like it was out before I knew how it sounded."

"It's all right, Dan. I've just been thinking about Sue. I don't really know her, but if you're sure she's your woman, that's all there is to say. If you have any doubts, why don't you break it up now?"

There were doubts, all right. Any man would have doubts after what had happened tonight. He put a hand to his cheek where she had slapped him, and the bitterness of that memory was a biting acid in him.

"Maybe that's the way it will be."

"I know how this has seemed to you," she hurried on. "What you said was blunt, but I'm afraid it's true. I might as well admit it. I've loved you for two years. I couldn't understand what had happened when you quit writing." She made a quick motion as if to wave it all away. "That's past, so we'll have to go on from here. You don't have to marry me to be Dad's partner."

"It might be the best part of the deal."

"If a woman really loves you, Dan, she will want what's best for you. I think that what Dad offered you tonight would be the best. Won't you think it over?"

"Sure."

"Would it be so bad if I went with the deal, Dan?"

"You'd make a mighty pretty wife," he said.

She smiled. "Thank you, Dan. Good night."

She swung away from him and went inside. He walked on to the barn, got a saddle blanket, and made a bed in the hay. He lay staring into the blackness, thinking of Quinn's offer. It could be done. Ash Lane, with a little luck and a lot of fighting, could be beaten, but it was Quinn's frank ruthlessness that bothered him. Lane had done a great deal for the country. In a way Reardon liked him, for he was honest in most things and to most people. Then Reardon thought of Collie Knapp, and temptation was strong in his mind. This was one way Collie might be saved.

Reardon was thinking about it when he went to sleep. When he heard Quinn feeding his horses he came awake at once, the decision still not made. He said, "Howdy, Pat," and got up, slapping chaff from him.

"Morning, Dan," Quinn said. "Sorry to wake you up, but we've got to roll. Say, will you go in and start that fire? Damned stove won't work for me."

"Sure. Astha up?"

"She wasn't when I left, but reckon she is by now."

Reardon walked out into the chill air and glanced up at the south wall, scarlet now under the morning sun. He crossed the yard to the cabin, thinking how well Astha would fit into his life, how much she had been at home last night; and all the loneliness and disappointment that filled his life were brought into sharp focus.

He opened the door and went in. Astha was still in the bunk. She sat up, blinked, and dropping back, pulled the quilt up to her chin. She said, "I went back to sleep, Dan. I meant to get up when Dad left."

"I'll come back—"

"Oh, I trust you. Just keep your back turned."

He went across the room to the stove, lifted the lids, and, taking out his knife, shaved off long splinters into the firebox. When the fire was going, she said, "You're an honorable man, Mr. Reardon. You can turn around now."

He picked up the bucket and looked at her. She was dressed and sitting on the edge of the bunk, her black hair down her back. "I'll get some water," he said, and went out.

When he came back she had combed her hair and was slicing bacon. She said, "Make the coffee, Dan."

Neither Astha nor her father mentioned the offer until Quinn had hooked up and they were in the buggy. Then Quinn said, "Well, Dan, you've had a night to make up your mind. I hope your answer still ain't no."

Reardon looked at the girl and ran the tip of his tongue over dry lips. He knew what he had to say. Right or wrong and regardless of Collie Knapp, he couldn't have any part in smashing Ash Lane. He said, "Still no."

He saw disappointment break across Astha's face, saw the anger that was in Quinn. It was Astha who said quickly, "I think you'll change your mind, Dan. Thanks for putting us up."

"Don't thank me," he said. "In this country company is always welcome."

"So long," Quinn said stiffly, and spoke to his team.

Reardon watched them wheel out of the yard. He turned back into the house and stood looking around, feeling the emptiness and the loneliness; and he wondered if he had made the wrong decision.

❧ CHAPTER 6 ❧

SUE Lane did not pull her horse down until she was out of the tamarack brush and on the county road. Only then could she control her crying. She could not think clearly. There was just the aching misery of an abused pride in her.

She reached Broken Bell, put her horse away, and walked quickly toward the house, not wanting to see or talk to anyone. When she glimpsed the glow of a cigarette in the darkness it was too late. Link Bellew laid his heavy voice against her. "Where've you been?"

"None of your business."

He reached out and gripped her arm. "Mebbe it is. I'm waiting till we finish Reardon. Then you'll get over him and marry me."

She tried to jerk away and could not. Suddenly frantic, she slapped him, crying, "I'll kill you before I marry you."

"I don't reckon so. You know how your Paw feels."

"He won't tell me who I marry."

"I know one thing as sure as hell. He'll tell you who you won't marry, which same is Dan Reardon. I've got a hunch you've been to see him."

"That's my business, too."

"I figger it's a little bit mine. Ash told Reardon tonight not to see you no more. That's where my part of it comes in. When Ash finds out you've been seeing him, I'll get the job of putting a slug into Reardon."

She kicked his shin, panic bringing the tears close again. He cursed in pain and let her go, saying he'd never seen a filly he couldn't tame. She ran on past the cotton-woods into the house. Ash was in his office, a small room off the big living-room. He called, "That you, Sue?"

She answered, "Yes," and darted up the stairs, afraid that he would follow and want to know where she had been. Only recently had he been asking her where she went. From the time the danger of the Utes had been removed, she had ridden wherever she wanted to in the valley, stopping to see some neighbor family, perhaps having a meal with one of them, and returning home after dark. She knew the valley like her own back yard; she knew most of the mesas and the lower ridges of the La Sals as well.

Running into her room, she slammed the door and leaned against it, panting. She was twenty, and for most of those twenty years she had felt as free as the wind. Some of the settlers had shaken their heads in disapproval, saying she needed a mother, that she was growing up as wild as an Indian. When Ash heard anything of the sort, he would grunt and say she rode like one anyhow and to hell with their advice. He didn't have a boy. If she wanted to grow up like one, it was her business, and the old women could damn well throw a loop on their tongues.

Now, for the first time in her life, Sue felt like a pris-oner. Ash had not said that she had to do her riding in the daytime, but he would. He had ordered Dan Reardon not to see her. The next thing would be to tell her she couldn't see Dan.

She felt her way across the room, found the bureau, and lighted a lamp. For a moment she stood looking down at the tintype of her mother. Ash had told her many times she looked exactly like her mother when they were married, but she remembered her mother as a faded woman with gray hair, tall and too thin, with a high, querulous voice. She had always been tired, always complaining, and always afraid of the Indians. Then Sue remembered what Dan had said. "Pretty soon you'd get to thinking about how it had been. All the things you'd had when you'd been home."

Other memories from her childhood came back, her mother saying in her bitter, nagging voice, "You couldn't stay in the San Luis Valley, Ash. You couldn't stay where I had decent furniture and a good house and people to talk to. You had to bring me out to this Godforsaken place."

Dan had been right! He was always right, and when she thought of that, her fury grew. She let down her hair and began brushing it in long, vigorous strokes, trying to forget Dan, forget what had happened tonight. She couldn't. She would never forget it. It would never be the same between her and Dan again. She turned her left hand and looked at the diamond, glittering like a fragment of ice in the lamplight. Then the tears came, and she could not hold them back.

It was not in her to wait, to play life safe. In that way she was like her father. She had heard Ash say time after time when he had stood staring up at the big picture of her mother in the wide gilt frame, "I couldn't stay back there, and she never understood why. I had to make something out of myself, and this was where I had my chance." She would go, willingly, Sue told herself, wherever Dan said.

She hated Link Bellew and his subtle way of influencing her father. Sometimes she hated Ash for his stubbornness and his arrogance, hated his love that gripped her with its possessiveness. Why couldn't he say, "I'll help Dan if he's the man you want." But Ash Lane would never say that, and she knew he would never forgive Dan for quitting his job and starting his own outfit. He found offensive in other men the quality that had brought him the wealth and power he held now.

She took off her clothes, suddenly hating them, a man's shirt and Levis, the high-heeled boots. Silks and velvets, fine lace and jewelry, candles and silver; those were the things a woman needed to round out her life, and she had none of them. Sure, Ash would buy whatever she asked for, but there would be no place to wear the clothes, no opportunity to dress up the table with silver and eat with the flickering light of the candles upon the table. They'd laugh and say she'd better go to Denver where people lived that way.

For a long moment she stood before the mirror, staring at her slim body, despising the dark tan of her face. Strange, she thought, that she had never noticed before how dark she was. She only noticed it now because of the pale softness of the rest of her skin. Suddenly, and she knew there was no sense in it, anger at Dan Reardon ran like liquid fire through her.

She put on her heavy flannel nightgown and threw back the covers. Returning to the bureau, she stood again in front of the mirror. Then she jerked the nightgown off and threw it across the room. She yanked out the top drawer of the bureau, picked up a silk nightgown, and put it on. She had bought it a year ago in the county seat. It had been the week after Dan had kissed her the first time and told her he loved her. No one knew she had it. She wondered bitterly if anyone would ever know.

It was a miserable world, a world of bitterness and hate, a world filled with great walls of pride as high and forbidding as the sandstone cliffs that rimmed the valley. Love was the one antidote for that misery, but she could not make Dan understand that. It was different with the valley wives. It had been different with her mother. Somewhere across the years love that perhaps had once been a rare and beautiful thing had wilted under the pressures of daily living. The difference was that she would not let hers and Dan's love wilt.

She blew out the lamp and slid into bed. The blankets were cold. She shivered, for there was no warmth in her nightgown. Drawing her knees up against her breasts, she hugged them to her. Outside, the hum of talk from the bunkhouse died. Ash clumped up the stairs, yawning loudly. She saw a gleam of light under her door. It died, Ash's door was pulled shut, and presently she heard the squeak of bedsprings as his great body was lowered upon them. Then there was silence.

Warmth slowly crept into her body, and she felt the tug of her old impatience. She lived again in her thoughts the minutes she had been with Dan, his kisses and the strength of his arms, their talk about Collie Knapp. The flame of anger burned in her again. She thought wildly, "He's put his crazy loyalty to Knapp above his love for me."

Then she was remembering her words, "Here I am, Dan. Take me." He had said nothing. She could not tell, even now as she thought about it, what had been in his mind, the reason for his hesitation, but she remembered hurrying on, "We'll go to your cabin, Dan. We don't care about the scandal."

He had said, "No." The word was like a knife in her heart. She held her knees tighter, the diamond cutting into her skin, and she hated Dan Reardon for what he had done to her. Then, and she did not know why, another thought reached into her consciousness. *Dan had been right.* Another man, a weaker man, would have said yes. It had been Dan's strength and love that had saved her. She relaxed with that thought, and she slept.

It was daylight when Sue woke. She heard the clatter of dishes in the kitchen, the talk of men while they ate. She waited until she heard them leave the house, then she got up and dressed. Carefully she folded her nightgown and laid it in the bureau drawer and went downstairs.

Ash was still at the table, dawdling over a cup of coffee. He looked up, scowling, "Did you see Reardon last night?"

She brought the coffeepot from the stove and filled her cup before she said, "Yes."

"Don't do it again," Ash ordered. "I've told him not to see you."

She sat down across the table from him and laid her gaze directly on his face. "You can't keep us apart, Dad."

He pounded the table with his fist. "I'll keep you apart all right. You think I want a son-in-law who sides an outlaw like Collie Knapp?"

"You don't know that he is an outlaw," she flashed back. "He hasn't been tried and convicted, and you have no right to do it." Only then did she realize she was using Dan's arguments.

"Who the hell says I haven't?" Ash bellowed. "I'm gonna stop this horse stealing if I have to hang Reardon alongside Knapp."

"If you do that," she blazed, "I'll walk out of this house and never come back."

He let her see the hurt that was in him. "No," he said hoarsely. "Don't say that. I've got nothing to live for but you." He swung a big hand in an all-inclusive gesture. "I've worked to leave you something big, Sue. You've got to marry a man who'll go on with what I've done, not a man who takes an outlaw's side."

She leaned forward, her hands fisted. "I'm going to marry Dan. You can't stop me. If you really love me, you'll help Dan get started. The only reason he won't marry me now is because he thinks he doesn't have enough money."

"He's damned right, he don't," Ash growled.

"You talk about doing this for me. All I want is a chance to live my own life and marry Dan. You don't really love me or you wouldn't be so selfish."

He wiped a hand across his eyes, blinking as if she had struck him. "Selfish! I didn't think you'd ever call me that."

"The only reason you don't like Dan is because he's independent. When he was riding for you, you thought he was fine, but you've hated him ever since he quit. If he hugged you up like Link does, you'd say he was the best man in the valley."

Ash rose, leaving his coffee untouched before him. For a moment he stared down at her, long-beaked face held very sober. "I'll hear no more of that talk. Link is the man for you to marry. I'll die knowing that what I've done will be handled right."

"I'll kill myself before I marry Link," she said passionately.

He turned and stalked out of the kitchen. She sat motionless, her hands clenched so tightly that her knuckles were white. She heard the clatter of a buggy only dimly, heard Ash shout, "Howdy, Pat. Howdy, Astha. Come in and get warmed up."

Sue rose and went into the front room. The Quinns were not stirring from the buggy. Quinn said, "We don't have time, Ash. I came over to tell you I'd buy you out."

Ash laughed incredulously. "You're joshing, Pat."

"No, I was never more serious in my life."

Sue came out of the house and moved toward the buggy. She spoke to them and received Astha's cool greeting. Quinn lifted his hat, saying gravely, "Good morning, Miss Lane."

Ash turned, frowning as if puzzling over something that was beyond explanation. "Pat here aims to buy us out, Sue."

"Well, tell him he's wasting his time."

"Yeah," Ash rumbled. "That's right. This is my valley, Pat. I was the first white man in here. Why, you know damned well I wouldn't sell for anything you want to offer."

"There is the other alternative," Astha said.

Sue had ever known Astha beyond a greeting when she had gone to Gold Cup and met her on the street or at a dance, but she disliked her thoroughly. There was no reason for her feeling except that she had heard stories of Astha's driving ambition, of the Quinns' unscrupulous business tactics. They formed, according to the gossip that filtered out of Gold Cup, a partnership that couldn't be beaten. If there was something they wanted that could not be secured by Quinn's threats and wealth, Astha could do the job with her smiles.

Now, staring at the dark-haired woman, Sue felt a premonition of disaster grip her. She breathed, "What sort of alternative?"

Astha was smiling now, a smile that did not go deeper than her lips. "You understand that we would rather buy you out than break you."

"Break me?" Ash roared. "What kind of talk is this, Quinn?"

"I'm telling you, Mr. Lane," Astha said. "We're going into the cattle business here in the valley. We'll be driving our own steers to the Gold Cup market in the fall. After all, it is our town."

"Well, I'll be damned." Ash stared helplessly at Sue. "Am I hearing this right?"

"You're hearing it all right," Sue said, tight-lipped.

Ash laid his gaze on Quinn's face, rage making his voice tremble. "I'm talking to you, Quinn. You're big as hell in Gold Cup. You stay there. Run your damned mine and your bank and whatever else you own, but you stay out of Long Tom Valley."

"No," Quinn said flatly. "I know this country as well as

you do. I figger it's as near cow heaven as any place in a hundred miles of here."

"Just where do you aim to start?" Ash snorted.

"With Dan Reardon. I'm backing him all the way, and you know I've got the money to do it. I'll have more cows in this valley than you ever saw."

"Reardon?" Ash began to tremble. "So that's it. First he throws in with horse thieves. Then he throws in with you. Why, I'll kill that—"

"I think not," Astha cut in. "Dan strikes me as a man who can take care of himself, and it will work out very well with us." She smiled at Sue. "You see, it will be in the family."

Terror brought a sharpness to Sue's tone, "What do you mean, in the family?"

"We stayed with him last night," Astha said maliciously. "Or perhaps it would be better if I said I stayed with him. We'll be married in the fall."

Sue walked toward the buggy, holding up her ring. "Dan and I are engaged."

"You've lost him," Astha flung back. "You can keep the ring or return it if you choose."

Sue dropped her hand, a chill emptiness in her. She could not doubt Astha. Suddenly she saw it. In blind rage she turned from the buggy and ran to the corral. She saddled her horse, her hands trembling, swung into the saddle, and rode out of the yard on the run, not looking again at the Quinns.

Cold air lashed at Sue's face, but she was not aware of it. She turned into the county road and followed it to the short lane that ran to Dan Reardon's cabin. He was working on the corral gate when she reined up in his yard. Dropping his hammer, he came toward her, grinning. He said, "Howdy, ma'am. Light and rest your saddle."

She stepped down and stood stiffly before him, struggling with her breathing. For a moment she could not make her tongue work. She would never forget the way she saw him now, his lanky long-boned body, his saddle-bowed legs. He had not shaved that morning, and stubble made his weather-burned face seem darker than it was. He had taken off his hat. A lock of brown hair was sweat-pasted against his forehead. There was a deep cleft in his wide chin; a faint scar slanted down his cheek to the right of his nose. All this she saw, a picture that impressed itself indelibly upon her mind.

"Can't you even say howdy?" Reardon asked, still grinning.

"Was Astha Quinn here last night?"

He stopped a step away from her, surprised, his mouth suddenly sober. "Why, yeah, she was here. How did you know?"

"I wouldn't expect you to tell me," she cried. "I guess there never was a bigger fool than I've been. I threw myself at you last night, but you didn't want me. I should have known."

"Maybe I'm thickheaded this morning," Reardon said, "but I don't know what you're driving at."

"Don't lie now." She stripped off the ring and threw it at him. It hit his chest and bounced off to drop into the dust. "You knew Astha would be here, so you couldn't bring one woman home when there was another one waiting. And I thought you were thinking of me."

"That's crazy. I didn't know she'd be here." Reardon put his arms around her. "I've got enough trouble—"

The tears were in her eyes again, blinding her. She struggled against his grip, beating at him with her fists, crying, "Let me alone. Haven't you done enough to hurt me?"

"I've never done anything to hurt you," he breathed. "I've never done anything for a year that wasn't aimed at fixing things so I could marry you."

He kissed her brutally, his lips hard against hers, but she was taut in his arms. He let her go, only then seeming to understand how she felt.

Her whisper barely reached him. "Astha's older than you, and if you'd been in the country very long, you'd know she's been married before, but if she's what you want, I guess you're old enough to know what you're getting."

"What is this crazy talk? I don't want her—"

"Do you have to keep lying to me?"

"I'm not lying—"

"All right, Dan." She swung back into the saddle. There were no tears now, but still she could not see him clearly. She was beyond feeling; her eyes could not seem to focus. "You said she spent the night here. I guess whatever Dad does to you will be less than you deserve."

She reined her horse around and rode slowly out of the yard, not looking back. She felt as devoid of life as a last-year's cottonwood leaf. Somehow she could not believe that all her hopes and dreams had been destroyed in these few minutes. But it was so.

CHAPTER 7

DAN Reardon stood like a man who had lost the power to move. *She had not believed him.* Love was not a thing to be torn apart and patched together. Either it existed between two people, or it wasn't there at all, and if it was there, faith would be part of it. But faith was not in Sue.

He picked up the hammer and a handful of nails. He drove a nail into the gate, missing it twice. He bent a second one and had to pull it out. No use. He dropped the hammer again and built a cigarette, staring at the Broken Bell buildings across the valley. Anger began to burn in him, the slow, smoldering anger of a man who does not lose his temper easily. Ash Lane had one thing he wanted. The next move, Reardon knew, would be aimed directly at him, and it would come soon.

Reardon was not conscious of the motives that drove him to his decision. It was largely the reaction of a desperate man reaching for anything that could save him. That, and the knowledge that there was nothing to stop him from fighting Ash Lane. The last bond between them had been cut clean. Then he heard the pistol-like sharpness of horses' hoofs on the Dolores bridge. The Quinns were leaving the valley.

Quickly Reardon caught up his buckskin, saddled, and mounted. Now that he had made his decision, he felt the necessity of getting it over with. He cracked steel to his horse and left the yard in a run, flashed past the store, and thundered over the bridge. Five minutes later he pulled up beside the Quinn buggy.

Quinn yanked on his lines. "You seem to be in a hell of a hurry, Dan."

"Yeah, I reckon I am," Reardon stepped down and moved to the buggy. "That deal still open?"

"Of course," Astha said. "I kept telling Dad you'd take it."

"How did you know?"

"Woman's intuition." She got out of the buggy and came around the back to him. "Maybe you think women aren't the same twice, but you'll find out one thing about me that's always the same. I know how you think."

He cuffed back his Stetson, suddenly wary of her. "I guess I'd better look out for you."

She wrinkled her nose at him and laughed. "You'd better. I'm after you."

"You won't have to chase me very far." Reardon turned his gaze to Quinn. "I've either got to draw or drag, Pat, and I'm not one to drag."

"I told you I'd back you all the way," Quinn said. "I'll get a bunch of gun slingers in here that'll finish Lane before the month's out."

Reardon shook his head. "If I'm going to run this end of things, I aim to run it. The kind of gun slingers you'd send from Gold Cup wouldn't do me any good, so I'll pick up a crew of cowhands. They'll shoot as straight as the toughs who hang around Gold Cup."

Quinn frowned. "Where'll you get 'em?"

"Utah. Pat, there's no use trying to make my Rafter R a big outfit. Not this year, anyhow. I can't buy hay in the valley and I don't have enough land to raise any more than I need for my horses."

"You've got to fight, Dan," Quinn said sharply. "The minute Ash Lane is busted, you can buy all the hay you want. Men are that way."

Reardon made a sweeping gesture. "Let's get one thing straight now. I don't want to bust Ash. I'll fight if I have to, but raiding Broken Bell, burning his buildings, and running off his stock just ain't my size. I aim to raise cattle."

Quinn's red face darkened with quick anger, but it was Astha who cut in. "He's right, Dad. Fighting just for the fun of fighting isn't what we want."

"What's your idea?" Quinn growled.

"How many steers can you market?"

Quinn pulled thoughtfully at an ear, looked at Astha and back to Reardon. "Well, it depends. A lot of the boys don't winter in Gold Cup, and I ain't real sure I can get everything tied up."

Reardon understood what he meant. To make his fight with Lane stick, it would be up to Quinn to organize the butchers in Gold Cup and in all the surrounding camps, or it wouldn't work. Then, in late winter with the passes closed, Quinn could ask the price he wanted for his beef.

"I savvy that," Reardon said, "but you'll have to make a guess. You're taking a long-odds gamble, Pat. You know that. Looks to me like you've got to bet it high and handsome, or you'd better pass it up."

Again Quinn glanced at Astha. She said, "Five hundred anyway, Dad."

"Yeah," Quinn said. "I guess five hundred steers."

"Can you build feed corrals this summer and buy hay

from the farmers down the river?"

"I figgered on doing that," Quinn said. "If I can't get my feed right, I'll send some boys out on the mesas and have 'em cut grass hay." Quinn drummed his fingers on the seat beside him. "Where are you gonna get five hundred steers?"

"Utah. They've got winter range over there, but we've got the summer range. I'll get over to Moab and pick up a herd, and I figgered I'd hire a few Mormon boys."

"Will they fight?"

"Sure they'll fight." Reardon swung his hand southward. "By the time we get 'em here, the grass'll be up. We'll throw 'em on the mesas. By October we'll be on our way to Gold Cup. The rest of it's up to you."

"I'll handle it," Quinn promised.

"Astha said it was your money against my cow savvy, half and half. That it?"

Quinn grinned. "Son, you might as well learn right now that what Astha says goes. If she said that was the deal, that's it."

"Now I don't want no part in your dealing with the butchers. That's up to you. I'll deliver the beef, and we'll figger they're worth a hundred dollars a head. I'll take my half of the profit the day the herd gets to Gold Cup."

"A hundred dollars a head," Quinn stroked his chin. "Can we make anything on that price, Astha?"

She was looking back up the valley, her face very sober. She said, "We'll make it, Dad."

For a moment Reardon saw the same ruthlessness in Astha he knew was in her fattier. Either they would make it, or the people of Gold Cup would do without beef.

Reardon said quietly, "I'd better have some money."

"Make it a blank check, Dad," Astha said.

"Hell, that ain't no way—" Quinn began.

"It has to be that way. Dan doesn't know what he'll have to give for the cattle or what he'll have to pay his men." She turned to Reardon, but when she spoke, her words were still directed at her father. "Some other man would cash that check for any amount he wanted to make it and get out of the country, but Dan won't."

"You trust me that much?" Reardon asked.

"Of course." Hesitantly she laid a hand on his arm. "You remember I go with the deal, unless you're still thinking of Sue."

Why not? Reardon asked himself. There was no use thinking now of Sue. A man had to take what his luck brought him, and Astha Quinn was better luck than most men had. He said, "You'd make a mighty pretty wife," and took her into his arms.

There was no hesitation about her now. She answered his kiss, her arms around his neck. In that moment there was no ruthlessness about her, none of the cool air of management he had seen in her when she had given quick prods to her father's hesitation. It was as if she had been waiting for this kiss all of her life, and the flame that was in her touched a spark to Dan Reardon.

When at last she drew away, she raised a soft hand to his cheek, whispering, "Dan, Dan, why did you wait so long?"

He could think of nothing to say. He wondered why she asked the question, for she knew that Sue was the answer. Then she must have realized she should not have asked it, for she added, "Don't tell me, Dan. You've been blind, but I knew how it was between us two years ago. It was worth waiting for."

Pat Quinn had busied himself with a cigar. Now he took it out of his mouth. "If you're done sparking—"

"It will be a long time before I see him again, Dad." She came around the buggy and got into the seat. "Let us know when you've got the herd into the valley."

"I'll let you know," Reardon promised.

Quinn put the cigar into his mouth and clamped down on it hard. "Just one thing, Dan. You've made your deal. I told you Astha was hell on promises."

"I don't go back on a deal," Dan said sharply.

"Of course not." Astha was leaning forward, her gaze lingering on Reardon as if setting the picture of him in her mind. "I don't know much about ranching, Dan, but I'll learn. Good-by." She shook her head. "I mean, so long. Good-by is too permanent."

"Good luck." Quinn handed Reardon a check, and spoke to his team.

Reardon stood watching them. Once Astha looked back and waved, and he waved to her. Then they were lost behind a turn in the road, and there was only the dust to remind him of what had happened.

Suddenly there were doubts. He had aimed to ask her whether she had been married before, and he had forgotten it. Well, it didn't make any difference. She had dragged her rope for him, but she had done it honestly and frankly with none of the subterfuges that so many women used. Mounting, he rode back across the river. Jess Vance stood in the doorway of his store. He raised a hand, sending his voice across the space between them, "How's things, Dan?"

"Good, Jess," Reardon said, and rode on. He knew the storekeeper was curious, but he thought it was better to let it go. Then, and only for a moment, did he let his thoughts turn to Ash Lane whom he still respected and even liked, to Sue Lane whom he had loved. The good times in the valley were gone for Reardon, the bad times were rushing in with the inexorable power of the Dolores as it swept out of the gorge to the south. He could not harbor regret; he had decided it this way.

For a long time Pat Quinn held his silence after they had left Dan Reardon. He looked sideways at Astha, seeing the sweet set of her lips, an expression he seldom saw on her face. Then, when he could hold it back no longer, he said with some admiration, "Well, you called it right down to a gnat's eyebrows."

She laughed. "Of course. Did you think I wouldn't?"

"You're damned right I did. Looked to me like a long shot if I ever saw one."

"I knew what Sue would do. She couldn't let it go, so she rode over to Dan, and he told her I'd been there last night. I'll bet she didn't even listen to his denials."

He chewed on his cigar a moment before he said, "Ain't you a little hard on the boy?"

"Hard?" She looked at him, surprised. "Of course not. I'll marry him, and I'll see he gets what he wants. Sue never could. That's what comes of having your father on your side."

"You think he'll forget her?"

"I can make a man forget any woman," she answered with cool certainty.

He stared ahead at the seemingly endless trough of the valley. "You're damned confident," he said. "Have you told him about Mark?"

"No. Why should I?"

"He'll hear, and then there'll be hell to pay."

"By that time we'll be married, and nothing can take him away from me."

"You missed a hell of a long ways with Mark."

"It's the only time I ever failed. I was young, and you were to blame for what I did. Dan's different. I'll live with him out here for a while. Then I'll get him to Denver and I'll get a white collar on him. He's young enough for me to make what I want to out of him."

"I ain't so sure," Quinn grumbled. "He's a purty solid boy, or I miss my guess. You sure you love him?"

"Love." She whispered the word softly, nurturing the sweetness of it. "Yes, I love him." She pursed her lips thoughtfully and said as if to reassure herself, "Yes, I think I do, and if he doesn't love me, I'll make him. I'll give him so much he'll have to. I'll help him dream. We'll have the finest house in Denver. Maybe we'll go to Washington. Or Europe."

"Or maybe you'll stay in a two-room cabin in Long Tom Valley."

"No, I won't. You'll see."

Quinn pulled hard on his cigar, wishing he could feel the certainty that was in his daughter.

CHAPTER 8

DAN Reardon saw the Broken Bell horse before he reached his place. He cracked steel to his buckskin, coming into the yard on the run, pulled up, and swung down. No one was in sight. Wheeling, he lunged into his cabin, gun palmed. George Price, a Broken Bell hand, stood by the table. There was a pile of shavings against the wall behind him, and the smell of coal oil was a stench in the air.

For a moment Reardon stood motionless, finding it difficult to believe what he saw. He hardly knew the man, for Price was one of several riders Bellew had hired after Reardon had quit Broken Bell.

Price began edging away from the table, right hand slowly working toward his gun. Reardon said, "Don't do it, George. Come out here."

Price licked dry lips. "Take it easy, Dan."

"Come on." Reardon stepped back through the door. "You make a wrong move and I'll kill you."

Price obeyed, still watching Reardon warily. Reardon walked to his horse, mounted, and riding over to Price's animal, reached for the reins. He said, "Start walking, George."

"Where?"

"Broken Bell."

"Link'll kill you," Price blurted.

"Maybe. Start walking."

Without a word Price turned and strode down the lane to the county road. An hour later they came to Broken

Bell, Price hot and dusty and inwardly raging, Reardon leading the man's mount. He called, "Ash." When Lane came out of the house, Reardon asked, "Bellew here?"

Ash scowled. "No. What are you doing on Broken Bell?"

"Bringing a man and a horse back. I should have shot the man."

Lane crossed the yard to Reardon, still scowling, his eagle-beaked face holding the hatred he felt for Reardon. He said, "You ain't welcome here."

"I don't like the smell myself," Reardon said, "but I'm telling you, Ash. Don't try to burn me out again unless you want the same dose."

"Who the hell's trying to burn you out?" Lane roared.

"Tell him, George," Reardon said.

"I did, Ash." Price looked at Lane defiantly. "Link's orders. I'd have got it done, and I'd have plugged Reardon to boot if I hadn't been in too much of a hurry to watch for him."

"I didn't figger you'd get that low down, Ash," Reardon said hotly. "I always kind of liked you. Much as I could like anybody who's too big for his pants."

Lane's eyes narrowed and took on that chill glint Reardon was beginning to recognize. He said, "You're drifting, Reardon. I'll buy you out, lock, stock, and barrel, or you can walk off and leave your outfit. Which way do you want it?"

"Neither. Remember what I told you. Burn me out and you've got trouble." Wheeling his horse, Reardon rode off, his back a tall, straight target. It was, he knew, the kind of boldness Ash Lane admired.

He tarried briefly in his cabin, gathering supplies and some of the things he wanted to keep—a tintype of his mother, Astha's letters, and the odds and ends that a man gathers over the years and that have value to no one but him. He had only a few letters from Sue, all written nearly a year ago when she had gone to the county seat. For an instant he stared at the envelopes, turning them over and noticing the way she wrote his name in big, bold letters. He knew what they said, for he had read them time after time until he could almost repeat them from memory. Quickly he turned to the stove and dropped them in.

Reardon brought up his pack horse and loaded the things he had set out. Mounting, he rode toward the south wall, not looking back. He understood this country and its people who were so much the product of Ash Lane's domineering will, so he knew what to expect. Later, if he died and Lane lived, there might be regret in the man, but there was none now. Only the stubborn pride of a man who cannot be diverted from the one thing he has set out to do.

Reardon could not condemn Lane, for that was the way the man was made. Then Reardon remembered what Sue had said about two bulls fighting. Now, climbing the twisting trail to the south rim, he saw clearly that it was the way Sue had said. There was no answer to it, no other way. Fight it out and hope to survive. Dan Reardon could do nothing else, for that was the way he was made.

Reardon reached Collie Knapp's place shortly after noon. Knapp came out of the cabin when Reardon called, a book in his hand. He asked, "Where you going with that pack animal, son?"

"Utah," Reardon said, and stepped down.

"Come on in. I've still got some trout. Had good luck last night."

Reardon watered his horses and put them into the corral. By the time he reached the cabin Knapp had built up his fire and was frying fish. Without turning, he said, "Trouble, trouble, trouble! What is it now?"

Reardon dropped into a chair by the door. He told Knapp about breaking up with Sue, about Quinn's offer and his acceptance of it, and about Astha. By the time he finished, Knapp had plates on the table and had poured coffee.

"So now you're into it," Knapp said softly. "Isn't it hell?"

"It had to come."

"Not if I'd stayed out of this damned country."

"I always make it a rule to play my hand the way the cards fall, Collie," Reardon said soberly.

"But I'm not important. I'm—I'm—" Knapp waved it aside. "Oh, hell, no sense talking about me. It's you we'd better talk about. You're making a mistake letting Sue go. I know how it'll be. You're thinking Astha will do, but some night you'll wake up with her in bed beside you, and you'll hate yourself and you'll hate her."

"I made a deal," Reardon said stubbornly.

"And you'll hang to it and fight until they kill you. In this country nothing works but force. A pair of hard fists and a fast gun. It's not the way to build a country, Dan, and it's not the way to be happy."

Reardon sat down and, reaching for the platter of trout, scooped one into his plate. "That's the way we live out here, Collie. It'll be a long time changing."

Knapp took the chair across from Reardon, handsome face shadowed by worry. "If I wasn't here, you wouldn't be having a controversy with Lane and you wouldn't have quarreled with Sue. But it's no good asking you to back up, so we'll take things the way they are. What can I do?"

"I hoped you'd go to Moab with me. I'll need you, and it ain't safe for you here."

"Sure, I'll go. I'm no cowhand, but I can cook." He frowned as if a new thought had struck him. "Say, you and I can't handle that many cows. Where are you going to get hands?"

"I'll hire some Mormon boys."

"They won't come if they know there'll be a fight with Lane."

"I figgered I could talk fast enough to get 'em. Maybe I'll have to pay 'em fighting wages."

"They won't come," Knapp said with conviction. "From what I hear, Lane used to buy feeder stock around Moab just like you're doing, and before he hired Bellew he gave some of the Mormon boys work through the summer. I don't think they'll have any part of fighting a man who's been friendly to them the way Lane has."

"How do you know so much about the Mormon ranchers?"

"I've heard the leaves whisper," Knapp said.

Reardon looked at Knapp, suspicion rising in him again, but there was no reading the man's face. Reardon said, "It's my only chance, Collie. The time to buy over there is now. The grass'll be up by the time we get 'em here. I could probably pick up some boys in Grand Junction, but it would take too long."

"I suppose it would," Knapp agreed.

There was no more talk until they were done eating and Knapp had cleaned up the cabin in his fastidious way. Then he filled his pipe, struck a match, and sucked the flame into the bowl, taking his time and covertly watching Reardon. He said, "Dan, I can get you four good boys. They'll fight, and they can handle cattle. I don't know what you'll have to pay them, but I think they'll be reasonable."

"I suppose you're going to pick 'em off a cedar," Reardon said with more sourness than he meant to show. "Look, Collie. I wouldn't even ask the valley men to take my side."

"These are not valley men." Knapp sucked hard on his pipe for a moment, scowling, brows pulled into a straight black line.

"Maybe you can get these horse thieves to turn honest," Reardon jeered.

"I don't know anything about the horse thieves, but there's one thing about these boys I'm mentioning. Don't ask them where they came from or what they're doing here."

"I reckon I don't need to know where they came from as long as they do their job."

"I'm not sure they'll take it, but we'll find out." Knapp looked around the cabin in the way of a man who never expects to see it again. "Well, Dan, it's been good. I have achieved a peace here I never thought I would find, but I have done it by withdrawing from society." He frowned and shook his head. "I know it's a coward's way, and I know it isn't your method of meeting a problem head on, but it's my way. The trouble is, a man can't lick anything by backing away from it." He took a long breath. "So I'll admit it licked me, and we'll let it go at that. Saddle up, will you, Dan? And bring my pack animal."

They left the clearing an hour later, Knapp taking the lead. They headed south, crossed the mesa, and followed a narrow trail down the side of the canyon to Deerhorn Creek. It was a small stream, moving sedately through its channel, its beaver ponds rich with trout. Once Knapp hipped around in the saddle, saying, "One of these days there'll be a thousand people in these parts and they'll clean this creek out. I'm glad I was here before it happened."

He turned back and rode on. Reardon made no answering remark. For all of the hours he had spent with Collie Knapp, there was much about him he did not understand and he never would. He only knew that Knapp's thoughts plowed deeper than any other man's he had ever known. He knew, too, that there was a scar upon his friend's heart that no amount of time would remove. Still, whatever it was, it had not made him bitter; it had not killed his ability to find pleasure in little things.

For an hour they followed the creek. Twice they jumped deer that leaped away into the brush, looking back as if in wonder. Then Knapp swung up the south side of the canyon, reached the top again, and wound through the aspens, angling gradually westward. It was late afternoon when they reached a red sandstone cliff, as sheer and deeply colored as the walls of Long Tom Valley.

Knapp reined up and sat his saddle, whistling loudly and without tune. He glanced at Reardon, winked, and said, "I guess it's safe. Anybody else riding in here would be shot to ribbons by now."

They went on, following the cliff for fifty feet, then swung directly toward it. Reardon knew this country, but he was not aware of the opening in the wall until Knapp reached it. He ducked his head to keep from being slashed by the brush. The notch was so narrow that he could have reached out and touched the sheer cliffs on both sides. It was deeply shadowed here, but a moment later they came into a bowl perhaps a hundred yards across. The chill of evening was in the air, although the sun had not yet dropped over the western rim.

There was a small fire built close to the east wall. Three men were playing cards beside it; another man, a Winchester cradled in his arms, came sliding down from his perch atop the rim.

They called, "Howdy, Collie," as if his visit was no surprise. The three at the fire laid their cards down and rose, suspicious eyes on Reardon. Then one of them, the stocky green-eyed man who had been at Knapp's cabin, said, "Well, it's friend Reardon. Light and rest your saddles."

The man with the Winchester stopped, called down, "All right, Frisco?"

"Sure, Monte. Go on back." Frisco grinned at Reardon. "You know, friend, I damned near plugged you at Collie's place. Good thing he rode in."

"I was glad to see him for a fact," Reardon admitted, and swung down.

They laughed, and Knapp said, "Dan, I want you to meet Frisco Hall under different circumstances than you did the other day."

Hall stepped up, his hand extended. "Collie's friend is our friend, Dan."

There was none of the panicky expression on the man's whiskery face that Reardon had seen before. His grip was firm; his eyes met Reardon's squarely. He motioned to the other two. "This is Hap Talley and Boomer Shay."

The Wild Bunch! Familiar names, all but Hap Talley, nearly as familiar as Butch Cassidy or Kid Curry would have been. Boomer Shay was a banty of a man, barely coming to Reardon's shoulder, with a knot head and small ugly features that seemed crammed too closely together. He was the oldest of the three, probably forty. Hall, Reardon guessed, was in his early thirties, and the other one, Hap Talley, was hardly more than a kid, certainly not over twenty-one.

Shay gave Reardon's hand a quick shake and stepped back, yellow eyes jerking furtively in their sockets to Knapp and back to Reardon, but there was nothing furtive about young Talley. Grinning, he said pleasantly, "Glad to know you, Reardon." He was slender, almost skinny, but good-looking in a way that would bring the eyes of any girl to him on a dance floor. There was a patch of freckles on his nose and cheeks; his eyes were light-blue and echoed the smile his lips held. A good kid, Reardon thought at once, who had fallen for the lure of easy money and thrown in with the wrong crowd.

"You boys hungry?" Hall asked.

"We'll eat when you do," Knapp said. "I filled Dan up on trout before we left home."

"Pull off your gear," Hall said, "and sit in on a few

hands. It gets kind o' monotonous after a while, just playing with a couple of boys that you know like you know your own self. Why, I can tell what they're holding when they raise me ten dollars."

There was good grass in the pocket, grass that was far ahead of that on the mesas, and a spring that ran a small stream through the opening by which Reardon and Knapp had entered the pocket. As Reardon offsaddled, he saw the Star Y horse that Hall had ridden to Knapp's place. When he returned to the fire, he said, "You'd better get rid of that horse, Frisco."

Hall grinned. "I aim to when I get a chance. You know, I was lucky to get him. I'd just come over the plateau, riding too damned fast, when my sorrel quit. Then I seen a fire up ahead. I walked in like I knowed the boys and made a dicker. I wasn't in no shape to auger."

"Star Y is over on the Uncompahgre," Reardon told him, "and some outfit grabbed off a bunch of horses and fogged 'em through the valley the night before I saw you."

"I guessed that," Hall admitted, "but like I said, I wasn't in no shape to auger."

Reardon told him about stopping Lane and his Broken Bell crew, and added, "If they'd found that horse in Collie's corral, they'd have had themselves a party."

Hall nodding, sobering. "I didn't tarry. I had a hunch it might happen."

"Ash Lane has an idea he wants to hang me anyhow," Knapp said. "He thinks I'm in with the horse thieves."

Hall laughed. "He sure pegged you wrong, didn't he, Collie?"

"The trouble is he won't listen to reason." Knapp hunkered beside the fire. "Let's see what kind of a hand you've got for me, Boomer."

Shay nodded at Reardon. "Want to sit in?"

"I'm broke," Reardon said.

Hall reached into his pocket and brought out a handful of gold eagles. "These will do for chips. We just play for fun. After I get all the dinero, we divide it up again."

"Distribution of wealth," Knapp murmured. "Too bad we can't all play like that."

Reardon took his place in the circle and played until the sun dipped behind the rim. He said, "I'm broke again, Frisco."

Hall rose and, scooping up the gold, dropped it into his pocket. "Time to eat. Boomer, take Monte's place. Hap, rustle some wood. Gonna be cold again tonight."

"I'll give you a hand," Reardon said, and followed young Talley to a deadfall pine that had crashed into the pocket from the rim above.

It was almost dark when they returned to the fire with armloads of wood. "We've got enough cut to last till morning," Talley said. "This hombre's a good hand with an ax, Frisco. We'd better hire him permanent."

"We don't need to hire him," Hall said. "We'll let him help us hold up a bank. Easy money and a long ride, Dan. Beats nursing a bunch of cows that somebody might steal from you."

"A long ride," Reardon agreed, "but there's always a chance a man won't finish it."

"That's what I tell them," Collie said. "More gold than they know what to do with and the only way they can spend their time is playing poker."

Hall grinned. "Now quit preaching, Collie. You ain't gonna reform us. The only time I ever reformed was during a camp meeting back home in Kansas. The organ player was a right purty blonde."

"Didn't last, did it?" Talley jeered. "You can't trust blondes. Now if she'd been a redhead—"

"Don't tell us about your redhead again," Hall groaned. "Hey Monte, come over and meet Dan Reardon. Dan, this keg of lard goes by the handle of Monte Denboe, but the chances are his ma called him something else."

Denboe came around the fire, grinning broadly. "Howdy, Dan. Welcome to Knapp's Hole."

Reardon shook Denboe's hand. He was a medium-tall man, pudgy of body, with a scraggly brown beard and a pair of dark-blue eyes. It was a strange thing, Reardon thought, how thoroughly they accepted him on Collie Knapp's say-so, yet there could not be anyone more different from them than the scholarly handsome-faced Knapp. As he had said before they'd entered the pocket, anyone else riding in would have been shot to ribbons. Reardon had never known an outlaw before, but with the exception of Boomer Shay, he would not have taken these men for outlaws if he had met them under other circumstances. Even Frisco Hall, rested now and momentarily safe, was pleasant enough.

Knapp said nothing about working for Reardon until after they had eaten. Then, with Frisco Hall shuffling the cards again, Knapp said, "How would you boys like to do a little honest labor for a change?"

They stared at him a moment. It took that long for them

to realize what he had said. Then they laughed. They slapped their legs and bellowed. Denboe rolled on the ground and almost choked.

Knapp stood motionless at the edge of the firelight, nursing his pipe, quietly smiling. When Hall could get his breath, he shouted, "Wait till I tell Butch. That's the damnedest thing I ever heard of. When we labor, it sure as hell won't be honest."

Denboe sat up, wiping his eyes. "I'm all for honest labor, Collie, but I'd rather let the railroads do it."

"Nothing honest about the railroads," Talley said. "I figger I'm just getting what's due me when I take anything off a railroad."

That, Reardon thought, was typical outlaw thinking. He built a smoke, stepping back into the darkness so they could not see his face, for he knew he was not hiding his feelings.

"Now that you're done with your merriment," Knapp said, "maybe you'll listen. This job will give you a chance to take a few shots at Ash Lane, and it strikes me it would be the best hide-out in the world. I doubt that any lawman would think of looking around a cow camp for his men."

There was a long moment of silence then, the three outlaws looking at Knapp as they gave this thought. Finally Hall said, "You know, Collie, I wish you'd get down off your high horse and ride with us. We could use a man with your brain."

"Yeah," Denboe agreed, "what you said sounds like sense."

Knapp told them about his and Reardon's trouble with Ash Lane, about Reardon's deal with Quinn, and what

Reardon meant to do. He added, "I've been thinking this over all afternoon, and it occurs to me that by October you could forget about hiding out as long as you stayed clear of Wyoming."

"So we drive 'em to Gold Cup," Talley said. "I always wanted to see that burg. Any women there, Dan?"

"Plenty."

"Wouldn't interest Hap unless there were redheads," Denboe said.

"I reckon he could find a redhead," Reardon told him.

"Well, I don't guess any of 'em could come up to my Laramie gal," Talley said. "Say, that was a woman. Why, she could kiss a man—"

"And make him forget his own name," Denboe cut in. "Don't tell us about her again. I can't stand it."

Hall was saying nothing. He hunkered beside the fire, stubbly face thoughtfully sober, fingers busy with the cards. It was Hall who would make the decision, and Reardon, watching him closely, saw that he was considering Knapp's suggestion carefully.

"I like that idea of throwing a few slugs at Ash Lane," Denboe said. "I wouldn't ask for anything better than to notch my sights on Link Bellew."

"It'd be better'n sitting here and rotting," Talley said with sudden sourness. "Sounds' good to me, Frisco."

Hall looked at Reardon. "You say Gold Cup's a purty lively burg. How big?"

"Five, six thousand."

"And this Quinn hombre runs things?"

"That's right. Owns the biggest mine around there and the bank."

"Now that banking business is my meat," Talley said, winking at Reardon. "I ain't much on putting money in, but I sure like to take it out."

Still Hall didn't move from the fire. He was staring at the flames again, shuffling the cards time after time. He ordered, "Call Boomer down, Hap."

"Time for me to go up, anyhow," Talley said, and drifted away from the fire.

There was no talk until Shay walked into the firelight. Then Hall sketched briefly what Knapp had said, and asked, "How does it sound, Boomer?"

"Good," Shay said tersely.

Hall rose. "Then it's a deal, Dan." He held out his hand. "I'll shake on that. In case you didn't know, Frisco Hall's word is good."

Reardon gripped his hand, not sure what motive had driven Hall into making the bargain. "Just one thing, Frisco. I'm running the outfit."

"Sure," Hall agreed, "as long as you don't stick our necks into a loop. We'll start in the morning, but you and Collie will have to fetch the herd out of Moab. Utah ain't real healthy for us. We'll wait for you out of town a few miles."

"That's fair enough. About wages—"

Hall waved it aside. "We'll work free, Dana Give us plenty of grub and keep the law off our necks. That's all we ask. We ain't wanted in Colorado, but some of these U.S. marshals get around."

Later, after they rolled up beside the fire, Reardon lay awake wondering whether he had been smart or not. He had glimpsed something in Hall's face he didn't like.

Avarice! Greed! The lust for more and more money! He did not doubt that the four of them would work and stay with him until the herd was delivered to Gold Cup. But after that! Reardon could not guess what the outlaw had in mind, but he was sure of one thing. Frisco Hall had seen something more in this summer's work than free grub, a hide-out in a cow camp, and the fun of tangling with Ash Lane's crew.

❧ CHAPTER 9 ❧

THEY rode out of the pocket at dawn, Reardon taking the lead. The extra supplies had been hidden in the sand of a cave floor, and Reardon had agreed to fetch a good horse from Moab for Hall. The Star Y animal was too dangerous to keep.

It was a wild, rugged country. Slabbed tableland. Canyons crisscrossing the mesas, their sides strewn with boulders and dotted by scattered cedars. In places the scrub oak grew so thick that a jack rabbit would have had difficulty getting through.

There was little talk and no complaint, for these men had known what to expect. They camped on the south shoulder of the La Sals, and were on their way again with the sun a small red ring to the east. This was Utah now, the land dropping down from the mountain range in a long sweeping flat—monotonous desert gray that was broken here and there by clumps of piñon, black dots in a vast sea.

They came into the slick-rock country, red and orange and buff. It was hot that day, the sun hammering down from a brassy sky in late afternoon. Then Hall reined up, saying, "There's a water hole yonder. We'll wait here for you, Dan."

Reardon nodded and rode on, Knapp beside him. No trail now, just the smooth rock blown clear of dirt by a steady nerve-tightening wind. They followed ledges, dropped down steep slopes of dry washes, climbed out again, and came at last to a canyon with a small creek at the bottom as red as the sandstone cliffs on either side.

It was a familiar sight to Reardon, but it was new country to Knapp. Once he licked dry lips and swung a hand around in an all-inclusive gesture. "Look at those monoliths, Dan. Why, this is a land out of the Arabian Nights. Minarets! Spires! Obelisks! Arches! I keep thinking I'll see a roc and a flying carpet and maybe Aladdin and his lamp."

"Keep looking," Reardon said sardonically.

"You don't see the beauty of a country like this," Knapp complained. "The Lord must have worked a little harder than average when He made it."

"I'd say He was plumb tired," Reardon said.

At dusk they reached a ranch with hayfields on both sides of the creek. It was a different world; even the air seemed changed. Damp and sweet now. Instead of the dry, singed smells of the desert, it was filled with a fragrance of growing things. Spring arrived here weeks before it touched Long Tom Valley. There was a peach orchard and tall cottonwoods and roses beside the sandstone house. A stooped man waited at a corral, curious eyes on Reardon and Knapp until they reined up and Reardon stepped down, his hand extended.

"How are you, Eli?" Reardon asked.

The stooped man shook his hand, saying gravely, "I'm fine, Dan. How are you?"

"A mite thirsty," Reardon said, and introduced Knapp.

"Take care of your horses and come in," the rancher said. "Supper's ready."

"I want to buy five hundred steers," Reardon said as he walked beside Eli to the house. "Have you got 'em?"

"I've always got steers. They'll be here tomorrow. The boys are fetching 'em in now." He fastened skeptical eyes on Reardon. "Heard you'd quit Broken Bell."

"That's right. I'm buying for myself."

"I didn't know you'd done that well in a year."

"You'll have cash, Eli," Reardon said. "I'll go into Moab tomorrow and get it."

"I wasn't doubting—" Eli began.

Reardon grinned. "I thought I'd put your mind at ease. Just one thing. I'll need a few boys to help me get the herd lined out."

"You'll have them," the rancher promised.

Reardon was back the next night, money belt heavy around his middle. They began work at dawn, bringing in a small bunch of cattle from the main herd to the cutting-grounds below the house. Eli picked a steer and Reardon picked one, back and forth until it was time to drive up another bunch. Knapp watched, an interested spectator to a scene that meant only dust and sweat and sharp bargaining to Dan Reardon.

The deal was made; the herd started down the creek. Slowly at first until the cattle became trail wise. Reardon sent the Mormon cowboys back just below the water hole where Hall and his men were waiting. Within an hour the four men drifted up, nodding greetings and looking the cattle over. "They'll do," Hall said. "Only thing is I'm thinking Ash Lane might like to have 'em himself."

"I reckon he would," Reardon agreed. "We'll rebrand in the morning."

It was slow, dirty work with the sun still hammering down from the cloudless sky. The old brand was vented, Rafter R burned on. Dust and sweat, wood for the fire, swinging loops, and finally darkness with every man but Collie Knapp so tired he dropped upon his bedroll without a word. A rest needed by both men and stock, then the trail again.

"Satisfied?" Hall asked, riding the bay gelding that Reardon had brought for him.

"Plenty," Reardon said. "Looks to me like I've got the best crew in Colorado."

Hall grinned, pleased. "Funny, ain't it? Even young Hap's a cowboy down to his heels." He scratched at a whiskery cheek, staring ahead at the long line of shifting red backs. "I've been thinking of what Collie said about honest labor. Feels kind o' good for a change."

"Maybe it feels so good you'll stay with it."

Hall reached for tobacco and paper. "I reckon not. Only reason we signed on with you was just what Collie said. A lawman wouldn't look for us in a cow camp, but sometimes I wish it wasn't this way. Take Hap there. He's young enough to get out, but not the rest of us. Once you pick the fork of the trail, you've got to keep riding."

Day after day. Over the shoulder of the La Sals. Down the slope into Long Tom Valley, Reardon scouting warily ahead. They kept close to the south wall, Reardon knowing that Lane could not let this go. Hour after hour, and no sign of Broken Bell. It came in late afternoon, Link Bellew and five men breaking out of the willows of Long Tom Creek.

Reardon bawled, "Stay away, Link," and brought back the hammer of his Winchester.

Bellew's answer was a slug that whistled a foot over Reardon's head. Reardon fired and missed, and knocked a man out of his saddle with a second shot. Hall rode up, shooting. Bellew pulled to a stop, lifted the man Reardon had shot to his saddle, and rode away, the rest of his men stringing along behind him.

"What the hell," Hall grunted. "They quit easy."

"Too easy," Reardon agreed. "Looks to me like a damned fool way to play it." Hipping around in his saddle, he waved to Denboe who was riding point. He yelled, "Keep 'em moving," and turned back to stare thoughtfully at the dust Bellew and his men had raised.

"Maybe he aims for you to put some fat on these critters," Hall said. "Come fall, they'll be worth stealing."

"What do you know about Bellew?" Reardon asked.

Hall grinned. He said, "Plenty," and rode away.

They threw the herd into Reardon's pasture that night. The cabin was still standing. Reardon had expected to see nothing but a pile of ashes. After supper he rode to the store, leading the pack animals, and bought supplies.

"Looks to me like you're digging purty deep for trouble," Jess Vance said. "How'd you manage to swing a deal like this?"

"Quinn," Reardon said. "We're partners."

"So that's it," Vance murmured.

"Bellew knew we were coming?"

"Sure. He had George Price watching for you."

"He didn't hit us like he meant business."

Vance spread his hands. "Ash is laid up with rheumatiz. Mebbe if he'd been along, it would have been different."

Reardon looked sharply at the storeman. Vance in his roundabout way was trying to tell him something. Jess Vance's sympathy might lie with Reardon, but it would not be like him to say so. Reardon reached into the cracker barrel and brought out a handful. He put one into his mouth and stood idling beside the counter. Then he said, "Maybe Link aims to let Ash do his own fighting."

"Mebbe," Vance agreed.

He would, Reardon knew, say no more. Reardon nodded and went out into the darkness, eyes searching the shadows. Suddenly a horseman appeared from the tamarack brush, let go with a shot that crashed echoingly into the silence, and thundered by toward Broken Bell. The bullet splintered the door casing and sang the length of the store to bury itself into the rear wall.

Cursing, Vance ran out with his Winchester. "Where'd he go?"

"Back to Bellew," Reardon said.

Vance stood motionless, swearing in a tight, bitter tone. "I don't want in on this, Dan. You've raised hell."

"I reckon I have, Jess. And you'll have a tough time staying out."

Vance wheeled back inside without another word. Reardon mounted and returned to Rafter R, wondering if

Bellew intended to make a serious effort to stop him.

"We'll keep a guard out," Reardon said when he got back.

"You won't have trouble," Hall said.

"How do you know?"

"Bellew ain't got the belly for a real fight."

Reardon said, "We'll keep a guard out anyhow. I'll take it first."

It was a moonless night with clouds rolling up to hide the stars. The blackness was complete; there was no human sound. Still, a vague sense of uneasiness began working in Reardon. It was too easy. Then, near midnight, he heard horses moving in from Broken Bell.

Bellew's voice sailed out of the night, "Reardon, you there?"

"Stay back," Reardon yelled.

Instantly Hall and the others drifted up, Hall saying softly, "He won't come in."

"What are your plans with them cattle?" Bellew called.

"My business."

"It's Broken Bell's business. You know the rules. Ash don't let no herd that size move into the valley."

"Then move us out."

"We will," Bellew said.

There was the thunder of hoofs, the racing blur of horses coming in, and guns started to talk. Hap Talley cried, "This is what we've been waiting for," and fired. The beef, bunched beyond the corrals, moved away.

"Stay in close to the house," Reardon called, and began working his Winchester.

Broken Bell was in close now, hammering out their

shots, swinging around Reardon and his men. One of Bellew's riders rushed in too far, his shape a high blot in the darkness. Both Reardon and Monte Denboe fired. The horse whirled, saddle empty, and raced away. The man lurched up, took a wild shot at Reardon, and went down before Denboe's gun.

Talley yelled, "Come on and get it."

The smell of burned powder was all around; the hornet *zing* of bullets churned the air. A sudden gust of wind touched Reardon and chilled him, and for a moment he thought, *Bellew aims to wipe us out.*

Boomer Shay let out a wild rebel yell and ran around the back of the cabin, emptying his six. Bellew lashed his men with his tongue, high and bitter. They rushed in, keeping a stream of bullets hammering into the wall of the house, picking up the fallen man, and fled. Dropping flat, Reardon laid down his empty Winchester and pulled his Colt. Then he held his fire, for Broken Bell was gone, not even answering Hap Talley's derisive jeer.

Reardon felt the warm flow of blood down his left arm and knew he had been tagged in the shoulder, a shallow wound that was now hurting. Still he lay there, thinking about this. Again, as in the afternoon, it had been a senseless kind of attack. With his greater numbers, Bellew could have moved in for a siege. By noon every rancher and settler in the valley would have been there. Instead, Bellew had made a show, lost a man, and pulled off.

Inside the cabin a lamp lifted into life. Reardon yelled, "Put it out."

It died at once. Collie Knapp said in an aggrieved tone, "A man can't sleep with all that racket. I thought I'd read."

Talley laughed. "Collie, you're a handy man to have around in a fight."

Hall and Denboe were there then, and a moment later Boomer Shay drifted in from the darkness. Hall said, "I was wrong, Dan. I didn't expect that of Bellew."

"Still don't look to me like he meant it," Reardon said.

"I told you he didn't have the belly for a real fight. Next time we meet up with him, he'll be sitting behind a rock notching his sights on us."

"Not if we get to the rim first, he won't." Reardon stepped into the cabin. "Anybody hurt?"

"I lost a piece of hide between my ears," Hap Talley said.

"You mean a piece of bone," Monte Denboe jeered.

Reardon fastened a blanket over the window. "All right, Collie. Light up that lamp and get on with your reading."

Knapp obeyed, picked up his book, saw the blood on Reardon's shirt, and laid his book down again. "I'll fix that, Dan."

There was nothing boyish about Collie Knapp's face now. He was thoroughly scared, Reardon saw, but his hands were steady as he poured whisky on the wound and bandaged it. This was, Reardon guessed, the first time he had been in a fight, and it had not been a pleasant experience for him. He wrapped a bandage around Talley's scalp wound, and dropped into a chair.

"How do you like it?" Reardon asked.

"A pair of hard fists and a fast gun. That's all this country knows." He grinned, a tight-lipped curving of the mouth. "If I live, I'll learn this kind of life. If I don't, it won't make any difference."

Hall came in. "I don't figger they'll be back, Dan, but I'll sit the rest of the night out."

Reardon nodded. "Bellew's made his show. I think he's finished for this time."

Reardon had guessed right. There was no trouble in the morning. After breakfast, Reardon threw his small bunch of steers in with the herd, and started them up the trail to the rim. Reardon sent Knapp on ahead with the pack animals, and held the rest of his crew back to handle Bellew if he made another attack. Still there was no hint of trouble. When the last steer had reached the mesa, Reardon asked, "You seem to know more about Bellew than I do, Frisco. I want to know about it."

"Nothing to know," Hall said irritably. "He's just a damned crook. That's all."

Reardon let it go at that. Hall's words were, he thought, a strange indictment for an outlaw to make of another man.

ᘺ CHAPTER 10 ᕬ

REARDON sent Monte Denboe and Hap Talley back to the valley to drive his cows and yearlings across the river to the top of Garnet Mesa where they would require little attention through the summer. He stationed Boomer Shay on the rim to watch for Broken Bell, and, with Hall's help, drifted the herd back into the scrub oak.

As the weeks turned spring into summer, it became evident that Link Bellew was content to keep Broken Bell cattle off the mesa, and ignore Reardon, but in spite of the lack of trouble and Frisco Hall's often-repeated assertion that they would hear nothing from Bellew until they were on the trail, Reardon kept a guard posted at the two spires where the trail curled over the rim.

"We got 'em this far," Reardon said, "and I don't aim to lose 'em. If we keep Broken Bell off that trail, they'll have a hell of a time getting on top."

"You're an old woman," Hall said contemptuously. "I tell you Bellew ain't a man to risk his hide."

"I sleep better anyhow," Knapp cut in, "knowing we've got a man watching."

Hall took his turn guarding the trail, but he rawhided Reardon about his caution when he had an opportunity. Reardon was certain that Hall had known Bellew before, but the outlaw was closemouthed about it. The other three talked freely about everything except the reason they were holing up here on the Dolores. About train robberies in Montana and Idaho. Stage holdups in Oregon. A bank they had cleaned out in southeastern Washington. But nothing about Wyoming or why that was the one state they wanted to stay out of.

Gradually Reardon learned to know these men. He liked and trusted Hall the least of the four. The man was sharp and cunning, possessed of a talent for leadership, and there was about him an air of leashed violence that Reardon knew must sooner or later break into explosive action. Still, he obeyed orders, he was pleasant enough even when he thoroughly disagreed with his instructions, and Reardon never had reason to complain of his work.

Monte Denboe and Boomer Shay were cowhands who

had made a bad step and kept on making more. Shay was a hard-looker, a dangerous man when the chips were down, and the heaviest drinker of the four, but he never made trouble. Denboe laughed a lot and joshed Talley about his redhead and was the worst poker player in the outfit.

Just as Reardon instinctively disliked Hall, he learned to like Hap Talley. Easygoing, even-tempered, Talley might have been another young cowhand earning his thirty a month and beans.

Reardon never could put his finger on what had caused these men to become the outlaws they were. They had their own strict code that made them hate Bellew because of something they knew about him. They would, Reardon was sure, stick with their bargain until the cattle were delivered in Gold Cup, but the conviction remained in Reardon that Hall, at least, had something else in mind.

As the weeks passed, Reardon's respect for Collie Knapp increased. His past was a secret he kept without giving a hint of what it might have been. He did the cooking, he took his turn at guarding the trail, and he never discussed the four outlaws with Reardon, but fear was never absent from him. It had been evident after the night battle in the valley.

Through it all Reardon had the feeling that it was a moment of quiet, that disaster waited for the day when they would take the trail again. The cattle ranged deeper into the rough country as the grass played out. Reardon moved camp, first into the bottom of Deerhorn canyon, and later on to the pocket where Knapp had taken him the day he had met Hall and his men.

There were hot days, then wet ones as storms boiled up over the mountains. Lightning fried the sky with livid crackling flashes. Thunder boomed like great boulders crashing down a rocky canyon side. On these days they stayed clear of the big pines and gnarled cedars that grew alone.

Then, well along in July, Jess Vance laid an old Laramie, Wyoming, newspaper before Reardon one day when he had come down for supplies. Vance pointed to the black headline: *U.P. Robbed at Desert Wells.*

Quickly Reardon scanned the story. Four masked men had done an expert job and got away with forty thousand dollars in gold and currency. They had separated, but the sheriff thought they'd be captured before they made the Colorado line. Reardon tossed the paper back on the counter, wondering how much Vance knew and how much more he suspected.

"Well, Link ain't bothering you," Vance said. "Ash is still cussing his rheumatiz. Ain't been in the saddle all summer."

"Too bad," Reardon said, building a smoke as he waited for Vance to go on.

"Funny thing," the storekeeper said casually. "Link keeps quizzing me about who you've got working for you. He says they shoot damned straight. George Price was wounded that first afternoon you got to the valley. Then that night Benny Lang was killed."

Reardon sensed that Vance was making some long guesses and that Bellew knew even less. He said, "I need some salt, Jess."

Vance came out from behind the counter, scowling.

"Link knows I've been selling supplies to you, Dan. He don't like it."

"Then tell him to stop me," Reardon said sharply.

"Link's too smart to try stopping you," Vance grunted, "but he'll stop me. That's the part I don't like." He rummaged in the pigeonholes in the back that served as a post office. "Got a letter here somewhere. Came three, four days ago."

He found it and handed it to Reardon, then began getting Reardon's order together. The letter, Reardon saw with quick interest, was from Astha. He suddenly remembered he had forgotten to let the Quinns know he had reached the valley with the herd. Tearing the envelope open, he read the note quickly. Astha and her father would be here Saturday.

Reardon slipped the letter into his pocket. He said, "The Quinns are coming, Jess. You reckon Bellew will do anything to them?"

Vance shook his head. "I can't make out what he is aiming at, but if Astha's with her dad, I don't think Bellew will touch 'em. That'd be damned dangerous, even in Long Tom Valley."

"They'll be here the last of the week," Reardon said. "Give 'em horses and start 'em up the trail. We'll see they get to camp."

"Now you look here," Vance protested. "I'm a storekeeper. I ain't running herd on no greenhorns. If Link finds out—"

"Tell me one thing, Jess. Ain't you a mite tired of bowing and scraping around in front of Ash and wondering what kind of coyote trick Link is gonna be up to next?"

Vance swallowed and scratched his head. "Yeah, but that won't save my neck—"

"If you ain't willing to do your part in licking Ash, you don't deserve your neck saved. Same with everybody else in this valley. There ain't a man here who wouldn't like to get up off his knees, but likewise there ain't one who'd crack a cap on my side. It makes me damned mad when I stop to think about it."

Reardon walked outside to cool off, knowing there was no use to say more. It was the first time he had given voice to something that had been prodding him all summer. Everybody in the valley would benefit when Ash Lane was cut down to normal size, but Dan Reardon had to do the job with a bunch of outlaws and an Eastern man who had been mistrusted by every nester and rancher from the day he had first come. Later, when Reardon rode away with his pack horses, he was not sure what Vance would do when the Quinns came.

Reardon had reached the south wall before he was aware that a man was coming down. He reined up, thinking it was Link Bellew, but believing he must be mistaken. Pulling in under an overhanging ledge, Reardon waited until the rider reached the bottom. It was Bellew.

Reardon said coldly, "That's Rafter R range up there, Link. You ain't welcome no more than I'm welcome on Broken Bell."

Bellew reined up, lips flattened against his teeth. He stared at Reardon for a long moment, crafty yellow eyes probing Reardon. "I didn't get very far."

"What were you doing up there?"

"That's a damned-fool question for a man who's been

on this range as long as you have."

"I want an answer."

Bellew licked his lips and said nothing for a moment. Reardon had known him for three years, but he had never been as fully aware as he was now of Bellew's cold scheming way, of the animal-like cunning that was so much a part of him. There was, Reardon thought, no loyalty in the man. Whatever he did was for Link Bellew and no one else.

"All right," the Broken Bell man said at last. "I was looking for strays."

It was a lie, and Reardon was surprised that Bellew had thought he'd believe it. He said, "You think your cows would climb that trail just for the view?"

"Might. Besides, we maybe could use some of that grass ourselves."

"Link, the minute you start a cow up that trail, you'd better get ready to butcher."

Bellew shrugged. "We'll see." He grinned, malicious triumph creeping into his yellow eyes. "You heard about Sue and me?"

"I don't want to hear it." Unreasoning anger washed through Reardon. What Sue Lane did was no business of his, yet the thought of her marrying this man sent a killing rage through him. "Link, I'm gonna recite chapter and verse to you. You tried to fire my cabin. You burned powder twice when we first hit the valley. Don't try it again."

The foreman's lips lost their grin. Yellow eyes narrowed. "You're taking purty big steps for a gent your size, Reardon."

"Maybe I ain't so little. Maybe you'd like to cut me down some."

It was a direct challenge. Bellew, Reardon knew, was a killer, but he hesitated now. The idea of pulling against Dan Reardon did not appeal to him. He was a man who lived by careful and crafty planning, and in the past his subtle scheming had been enough. It was not good enough to handle Dan Reardon.

Bellew sucked in a long breath, his face going red. He blurted, "You've thrown in with Collie Knapp, and we know what Knapp is. If he'd help horse thieves, he'd rustle cows. One of these days I'm coming up on the mesa to have a look around."

"Then you'd better come smoking."

"I will when the sign's right."

"Maybe this would be a good time."

"I pick my time."

"I always figgered you had a yellow streak."

Suddenly Bellew's control broke. The red had gone out of his face. He was white and nearly crazy. He shifted in his saddle so that he could reach his gun easily; he was sucking in his breath with long gulps. He ground out, "I'm done fooling, Reardon. This range is too small for both of us."

"You talk too damned much," Reardon breathed.

For a moment Reardon thought that this was it. Then the sound of a horse on the trail above came to them, and Bellew turned in the saddle to look. He cried out in a thin voice, "There'll be a day, Reardon, but it won't be when you have a man planted behind me."

Bellew cracked steel to his horse and rode off. Reardon

stared after him, knowing that the time would come when he must kill him, and regretting that this had not been the day. The hope would not leave him that if Link Bellew was out of the way, Ash Lane would be different. He turned his buckskin up the trail. Collie Knapp was coming down, Winchester held across his saddle. He reined up when he saw Reardon coming up the trail.

"What'd you horn in for?" Reardon called angrily when he reached Knapp.

"Looked like a row," Knapp said nervously.

"It was," Reardon said, still angry. "I never saw the day I couldn't handle that ornery son."

Knapp looked down, troubled. "I'm sorry, Dan. I guess I just don't know how to do things out here."

Reardon was ashamed then. He said, "It's all right, Collie. Were you on the rim when Bellew rode up?"

Knapp raised his eyes, hesitating a moment before he answered, "Yes. I wouldn't let him go on."

Reardon nodded approval. "Maybe you know more about how to do things than you figger. What did he want?"

Again Knapp hesitated. "I don't know. He said something about looking our cattle over for Broken Bell strays."

"Hell, that was just a stall. Well, let's get back up."

Afterward, riding to camp alone, Reardon wasn't sure that Knapp had told him all there was to tell. It was the first time he had sensed an evasiveness in him. Then his mind turned to the Quinns, and he forgot about Knapp. He did not look forward to seeing Astha with as much pleasure as he should. That, he told himself, was a hell of a way for a man to feel about the woman he was going to marry. The sooner he pushed Sue out of his mind the better.

❧ CHAPTER 11 ❧

REARDON, watching from the rim with young Hap Talley, saw a dust cloud far up the valley. "That'll be the Quinns," he said. Later the buckboard emerged into view and, crossing the bridge, stopped at Vance's store.

"They think they can get up here in that rig?" Talley asked. "Hell, they'd better sprout wings."

"Pat didn't know where we were," Reardon said. "I was supposed to let 'em know we'd got here, and I forgot it."

Talley looked at Reardon sharply. "That's your girl down there, ain't it?"

"Yeah." Reardon grinned wryly. "I reckon I'm in for it."

Talley held his silence then, not understanding, and Reardon did not explain. He could not have put it into words if he had tried. He had never thought of writing to Astha when he was at the store, but actually it was not a matter of forgetting. More than once he had taken out paper and pencil when he was idling around the campfire at night, but he had never succeeded in putting any words down. They had refused to come. He was wondering now what he could say to Astha to make her understand.

Reardon watched Vance saddle up two horses. Presently Astha and her father mounted, rode toward the foot of the trail, and started up. They moved slowly, resting often on the switchbacks. Neither, Reardon thought, was used to riding.

It was nearly noon when the Quinns topped the rim. Reardon lifted his hat, calling, "Howdy, Astha. Howdy, Pat."

"Howdy," Quinn called back.

Astha reined up and looked down at Reardon. She said flatly, "I'm awful mad at you."

"You've got a right to be," Reardon admitted, and held up his arms to her.

Astha slid out of the saddle. Reardon caught her and lowered her to the ground, but he did not let her go. He had forgotten how good-looking she was; he had forgotten the dimple in her right cheek when she smiled, and she was smiling now.

He pulled her to him and kissed her, and she responded with a fervency that made Talley's eyes widen. When Reardon released Astha, Talley let out a whoop. "By grab, I'd like to have a woman mad at me thataway."

They all laughed, even Pat Quinn. Reardon said, "This is Hap." He remembered in time that Talley might not want his name known, and added, "Jones. One of our riders. Hap, meet Pat Quinn. And Astha."

Talley shook Quinn's hand and lifted his Stetson to Astha. "Dan told me about you, ma'am, but he didn't say you was so d—, I mean, purty. I don't know what you see in that long-legged son, but there ain't no doubt about what he sees in you."

"I see plenty in him, Hap," Astha said quickly, "but he's been neglecting me something terrible. I haven't heard from him all summer."

"I'll loan you my gun if you want to shoot him."

Astha wrinkled her nose, smiling. "I'll remember that. I might need it to get him in front of the preacher next fall."

"How's the cattle?" Quinn broke in.

"Fine," Reardon answered. "Five hundred like you said, and I threw in my bunch. Twenty of 'em. I didn't ask you about that, but I figgered we might lose a few."

"Sure," Quinn said. "We'll allow you full price for yours. I'll use all you can fetch. Gold Cup is on the boom. I just opened up a new mine in Easter Basin. Made the strike right after we were here last spring. That means another thousand men will be wintering in Gold Cup."

"Why, now, that sounds good." Reardon looked at Astha. "Hungry?"

"I can eat."

"We're camped quite a piece from here. Knapp's Hole, the boys call it. I guess Collie found the place. I didn't know if you'd want to ride that far."

Astha rubbed her seat ruefully. "I never knew a saddle could be so hard," she said.

"We want to go to your camp," Quinn said. "I'd like to see our cows."

"Then we'll eat at Collie's cabin and take the rest of the day getting to camp." Reardon nodded at Talley. "I'll send Monte out in the morning."

"You'd better." Talley still held his gaze on Astha's face, admiration in his eyes. "It'd be a dirty trick to keep me here with beauty like that in camp."

Reardon helped Astha into the saddle. "Just remember one thing, Hap. I've got my brand on her."

Talley grimaced. "I'm always too late."

"You should be complimented, Astha," Reardon said. "Hap likes redheads."

"That depends," Talley said quickly.

Astha laughed. "On whether a redhead is handy, I suppose. I'll take care of that, Hap. When you get to Gold Cup, I'll have all the redheads out to greet you."

"I'll count on that," Talley said.

Reardon swung into saddle, and they took the trail for Knapp's cabin. Quinn said in a bragging tone, "I've got everything wrapped up, Dan. All the butchers are with us. They found out it don't pay to buck Pat Quinn in Gold Cup. Lane won't find a buyer if he gets his cattle into camp."

"I wasn't worried," Reardon said.

"Why didn't you meet us at the store?" Astha asked.

"Didn't seem like the smart thing to do," Reardon told her. "We've had a couple of run-ins with Broken Bell."

"Lose any men?" Quinn asked.

"No. We came out pretty well, but I don't get down off the mesa unless I have to go to the store for supplies, and I was afraid Bellew might take this chance to crack a few caps. I don't want you around when it happens, Astha."

Worry flowed across her face. "I'll be living here after we're married, Dan."

He didn't say anything for a time. He had thought of that, but it was too far into the future to give him concern. "I hope it will be over by then," he said at last.

"It will," Quinn said confidently. "I'll have Ash on his back before you're here, Astha."

"Dan, I don't like it," Astha breathed. "Your life is too

valuable to waste."

He grinned. "I've been lucky. Maybe I'll still have luck."

On the way to the cabin he told them about getting the herd in Utah and bringing it into the valley, and about the crew. "They're good boys," he finished. "It was luck finding them."

Quinn grunted approval, and Reardon let it go at that. Quinn was interested in only one thing, getting the beef to Gold Cup. How they got there and who brought them and the number of men killed in the process was immaterial. That became more evident as the afternoon wore on to dusk.

Astha said little, but her father talked a great deal, and as he talked, it became apparent to Reardon that there would be no permanent partnership between them, for Pat Quinn's ways were not his ways. The banker made no apologies for his tough tactics in organizing the butchers. He had ridden over them roughshod the same as he had ridden over all his opposition in Gold Cup, and he bragged about it.

Dan Reardon had grown up in western Nebraska. He had seen his father smashed by a ruthless, powerful neighbor. As a boy he had been taught to hate monopoly, and he hated it now. From the day he had made the agreement with Pat Quinn, he had told himself that beating Ash Lane was the only way that his hold on the valley could be broken. Now he saw, and it was knowledge that sickened him, that Quinn was far more of a monopolist than Lane would ever be. Lane was content to dominate the valley, Quinn was dipping into every field of business he could reach.

Now, riding beside Quinn, Reardon studied the man's red, muscle-ridged face, and dislike grew in him. Quinn was talking freely and frankly, obviously not understanding Reardon's feeling, taking it for granted that Reardon would go along with him.

"Before we're done," Quinn said, "we'll be the biggest men on the western slope. I'm going to the top, Dan, and I'll take you along. Before another year is gone, I'll control the railroad. Transportation is like the arteries of the body. It furnishes the lifeblood for any country." He chewed on his cigar, staring unseeingly into space. "Before I'm done, I'll be in politics. If you're rich enough, you can buy anything, and I aim to be rich enough to buy what I want."

Only then did the full truth break across Reardon's mind. It was like the searing heat of a flash of lightning. Pat Quinn was a maniac driven by his desire to gain wealth and power, and Dan Reardon would be a cog in his machine. Quinn needed him, and Astha had been the bait to bring him to their side.

They reached Knapp's Hole at dusk, the campfire an inviting red glow in the thinning light. Knapp and the others were there, calling greetings. They dismounted, Reardon introducing the Quinns. Boomer Shay took care of the horses, Monte Denboe was as hearty in his admiration of Astha as Hap Talley had been, and Collie Knapp announced with a flourish that supper was ready. Only Frisco Hall stood aloof, sizing Quinn up as coolly as a butcher would size up a beef.

"We've only got time to stay one day," Quinn said.

"You can show me the cattle tomorrow, Dan, and we'll head back the next morning." He winked at Reardon. "Fact is, I didn't have time for this trip, but Astha nagged me so long I surrendered. You'll get used to that, Dan."

"I nagged him." Astha sniffed. "What are you trying to do, scare him off, Dad?"

"I reckon he don't scare that easy," Quinn said.

Astha stayed in camp the next day, saying she didn't know there was so much of her that could get sore. Quinn rode with Reardon, making a wide circle through the aspens to the west, and returned to camp in late afternoon, warm in his optimism about the cattle.

"There's no end to this thing, Dan," he said thoughtfully. "Root Lane out of his hole, and we could handle ten thousand head. You won't have to go to Utah for them. We'll feed and winter right here in the valley."

"Ash won't root that easy," Reardon said.

Quinn laughed. "You'll see. Come winter, and Lane will be out of the valley."

Reardon said nothing, but he was aware of Astha's eyes on him, and he knew she had sensed what was in his mind. After supper she came to him, saying softly, "Let's take a walk, Dan. I haven't had a chance to talk to you since I got here."

They moved away from the firelight, Hap Talley grinning knowingly after them. When they were out of sight of the others, Astha stopped him, breathing, "Dan, you've kissed me only once since I came."

For a moment she stood facing him, her hands on his arms speaking for her. Then he brought her to him, and her lips lifted with quick eagerness to his. In that moment everything but this girl was blotted out of Reardon's mind by the shocking power of her kiss. When he let her go, she put her cheek against his, whispering, "Dan, Dan, it has been so long."

They walked on until the fire was a distant star in the night. She said, "Let's sit down, Dan."

She dropped into the grass and sat with her back against a boulder, eyes raised to the star-freckled sky. "This is the most beautiful place I have ever seen, Dan," she said. "Everything else seems far away, trouble and fighting and men's ambitions."

He built a smoke and held a match to it, the flame leaping into the darkness to throw a brief light across his dark face. He said then, "You mean your dad's ambition."

She pulled him down to sit beside her and leaned her head against his shoulder. "I knew what you were thinking, Dan. He is ambitious, but you shouldn't blame him. Ambition has brought him a long ways."

"He aims for it to take him a long ways farther," Reardon said dryly. "I didn't tell him, but maybe you'd better. I don't aim to go along."

"You told me once you wanted your own life, Dan," she reminded him. "Money's one way to get it."

"I don't think so. Looks to me like it's the same thing as whisky is for some men. Pat will never get enough."

"It isn't money he wants, Dan. It's the power and prestige that money can buy."

"Same thing. He'll never get enough." Reardon smoked his cigarette down and ground it out under his heel. Then he said, "I've been thinking. You've been used to a lot of people and fine clothes and a big house. You won't like living in the valley with me."

"I'd like living anywhere with you. Can't you understand that? Dad lives his life, and it isn't mine. I guess I'm the loneliest woman in Gold Cup. I want my own life, Dan. I want to make something of it myself."

She had phrased what had long been in his mind, something he had never been able to say. He sensed the tenderness that was in her as she pressed into his arms and brought his face down to hers. Again, for this moment, the world was a distant thing. There were just the two of them, and the future was a bright promise.

She cradled his head in her lap, a soft hand against his cheek, and she was saying, "I'll give you all of me, Dan. Everything, and I would ask nothing but your love. We'll build our lives together and we'll make our dreams."

Later, long later, they walked back to camp, his arm around her. *You take what life deals,* he was thinking, *and you play the hand for all it's worth.* He was, Reardon told himself, luckier than most, luckier than he deserved.

Before they reached the fire, she paused and faced him, saying softly, "It's been so short a time, but there's always tomorrow. I'll be living for that tomorrow. It won't be long until you're in Gold Cup, and we'll be married whenever you say."

She kissed him again and moved quickly away as if it was an effort to leave him. He stood motionless, watching her, and telling himself again he was luckier than a man deserved to be. Then he thought with striking insight that it was strange he had to keep telling himself that.

Knapp rode with Reardon the next morning when he took the Quinns back to the rim. They waited, watching

Astha and her father go down the trail and on across the flat to Vance's store. Still they waited, Reardon smoking and saying nothing until the buckboard disappeared in the hazy distance. They turned back, Reardon thinking with sour persistency of Knapp's words, "Someday you'll wake up in bed with her beside you and you'll hate her."

Funny he couldn't get that out of his mind. He could hate her father, but he could never hate Astha. He had seen men haunted and driven crazy by the memory of the women they had lost. It would not be that way with him. Time was the answer. He would forget Sue.

"She's a damned handsome woman," Knapp said, suddenly, "but she's also an ambitious woman. You're too stubborn to change, so you'll go ahead and marry her, but you'd better start getting used to the idea that she'll put on the pants the morning after you're married, and she'll keep wearing them."

"I made a bargain," Reardon shouted in a savage tone he had never used on Collie Knapp before. "Now, shut up."

"Sorry." Knapp gave Reardon an odd, probing look. "I'll never mention it again."

They rode back to camp without a word.

CHAPTER 12

FIFTEEN years in the valley had taught Ash Lane that July was ordinarily the hot month of the summer. On the mesas vagrant breaths of wind stirred the thin air; the nights were always cool and sometimes close to freezing, but the valley was entirely different. The great sandstone cliffs were like sides of an oven, harboring the heat until the next day's sun was in the sky. Thunderstorms brought the only relief, but there had been few storms this July.

Lane tossed a tally book down on his spur-scarred desk and brought himself upright, holding his weight on his right leg. His left, filled with misery in every joint, had given him more pain during the last three months than he had suffered in all of his sixty previous years. He looked around the cluttered room at the saddle and guns and odds and ends of leather. This was the nerve center of Broken Bell, the capital of an empire. It was Ash Lane's private domain in which even Sue did not dare move as much as a strap or a piece of paper. Lane loved it, but today he found no pleasure in it. He wiped his face with a red bandanna, wondering why he felt this way. *Probably the rheumatism,* he thought as he limped out into the front room.

Sue was not around, and the house seemed uncomfortably quiet, too quiet. Even an argument with Sue would be better than this pall of silence. He felt like a man living in his own tomb.

He looked around the familiar room that for some vague reason seemed strange to him now. The great oak table had been freighted in from the San Luis Valley, the one concession he had made to his wife. He thought, in a detached way, *I should have brought the other things she wanted.*

He lowered his gaze to the bear hide on the floor. He had roped the bear the first year he had been here and he'd had some fun with it before he'd killed it. He glanced at the great stone fireplace that filled the room with crackling heat when it was piled high with cedar. His wife had thought it was too big.

Again, as he had so many times these last weeks, Lane turned his eyes to his wife's picture on the wall. She had never understood the ambition that had driven him across the San Juan range to this valley. Now he pictured her as she looked the day they were married, a slim and shining girl, proud of him and proud of her body. She had been as pretty as Sue.

There had been a time when his wife had loved him. She must have, for there had been the good years, years when she had welcomed him with her kisses when he had come in at dusk, years when she had been all a wife could be. But she had liked the San Luis Valley, and he had hated it, and that had been the cause of their trouble.

She had come with him, even though she had argued against the move. They had driven their small herd across the mountains when Sue had been little more than a baby. First a small cabin close to the river. They had prospered, for the price of cattle had always been high in the mining camps to the east. He had built this house for her, but she had not liked it; she had not liked anything he did. She loved the broad sweep of the San Luis Valley with the Sangre de Cristo range on one side, the San Juans on the other, but she had despised the muddy Dolores, the tall sage, the red cliffs that were like a prison, the bands of Utes that drifted through Long Tom Valley. So she had died, hating Ash Lane because he had brought her here.

He limped to the porch and eased himself down into his rocking chair. He bit off the end of a cigar and fired it.

Leaning back, he began to teeter, his bad leg propped up in front of him on the porch railing, the squeak of the rocker rhythmical and soothing. Lifting his gaze to the south rim, he thought of Dan Reardon, the man Sue loved, Dan Reardon who defied him, and hate was a festering sore in Ash Lane. He told himself he could forgive all of Reardon's sins but one; Reardon had come between him and Sue.

Throughout his life pride had been a compelling force in Ash Lane. It had driven him across the mountains over his wife's protests because he had seen no chance to get ahead. The necessity of earning a living had required him to supplement his meager profit from his cattle by working for men he despised. They had been the first ones into the valley, so they had taken the best. Many of them were wealthy and had bought great pieces of the old Mexican grants.

Lane had scraped out a living, discontent growing in him. His best years were already lost. When a man is over forty, he has only one chance left before the last of his strength is gone, the last dream burned down to a black ember. Ash Lane was then forty-five.

So he had moved; he had been a success and he had no regrets. He took the cigar out of his mouth and looked absently at it. No, he was sure he had no regrets. He had done what he had set out to do, and now he reached into his mind for the satisfaction that had so often been his.

A man had a right to be proud of accomplishment. When Ash Lane spoke in Long Tom Valley, men jumped. When he told a neighbor rancher that his herd was too big, his neighbor pruned it down. When he told a settler how much he would give for a ton of hay, the settler took it. That was the size to which Ash Lane had grown, king-size like the men he had worked for in San Luis Valley. But there was a difference. They had been born with money; he had gained his by vision and determination and sweat.

For some reason the satisfaction did not come today. Instead his failures clung to his mind and grew to plague him. There was Collie Knapp, whom he had promised to hang, Collie Knapp, who scorned the valley and its people and their way of life. Dan Reardon, who had quit his job with Broken Bell to have his own ranch. And Pat Quinn, who had blandly offered to buy him out and, when he had refused to sell, had promised to break him.

For a moment Lane thought of the money he owed Quinn and he cursed his weakness for poker. He seldom played except when he was in Gold Cup, and last fall it had been disastrous. Fear sent a knifing spasm through him. He immediately drove it out of his mind, for fear was a luxury he never permitted himself. The amount due Quinn in the fall was about seven thousand, small change compared to what he would make from his cattle. Quinn had intimated that there would be no market in Gold Cup for Broken Bell stock, but Lane dismissed the threat as idle boasting. For years he had sold his beef in the mining camp, and the butchers were his friends.

He put his cigar back into his mouth and pulled on it. It was dead. He held a match flame to it again, still idly rocking. These failures, he told himself, were not serious, little things that time would cure. Collie Knapp and Dan Reardon would leave. It would have to be that way when Knapp lost interest in his lonely unnatural life and

Reardon failed with his cattle. Eventually Quinn and Reardon would break up. But Lane's real failure was with Sue, and he saw no way in which time could cure that.

Lane turned his glance toward the La Sals, still dotted by snow patches, to the old Ute trail curling up over the ridges. Then he looked eastward across the Dolores to the long reach of the valley. His valley! Broken Bell's winter range! Suddenly everything that he had done in the fifteen years that he had been in the valley seemed unimportant. Trivial. A house built on sand. From the moment his wife had died, he had worked for Sue, for the children that would be Sue's. That was his hope for immortality. But Sue wanted only one concession from him, and he could not bring himself to give it to her.

He was remembering the things she had said since she had broken up with Reardon—about his love being selfish, about the ruthless way he ruled the valley, about his failure to think of anyone but himself. Nobody, not even his wife, had ever talked to him as Sue had.

A sickness worked into him. He wiped his face with his bandanna, a shiver raveling down his spine. He denied everything Sue had said. His love for her was not selfish because he wanted her to have luxuries he had not even given himself. He ruled the valley for the good of all of them. He had kept the range from being overstocked. The settlers had a market at home for what they raised. If Reardon had his way, there would be a hundred families in the valley instead of a dozen, and most of them would starve.

But it didn't go down. He was honest enough with himself to recognize that these were excuses. He swore aloud, finding no comfort in honesty. No one had challenged his motives before; no one had a right to now. Nor did it help to know that Sue had stated a simple truth when she had said, "There's only one real reason you don't like Dan, and that's your fear that someday he will be as big as you are."

He threw his cigar butt into the dust of the yard. He had a right to hate Reardon for that reason; he had a right to live his life out as he had planned it without this threat of rebellion. He fumbled another cigar from his pocket and fired it, but the tension would not leave him. Whatever the right or wrong of it was, the one fact that a wall had risen between him and Sue was enough to destroy his peace of mind.

It was midafternoon when he saw Sue ride in from the south. He rocked steadily as he watched her dismount, pull gear from her horse, and let him into the pasture beyond the barn. She came to the house, walking briskly, and his love for her seemed to rise up and smother him. Then a sense of injustice rankled in him. She had no reason to feel the way she did. Reardon was not worthy of her.

Sue came past the big cottonwoods in front of the house and dropped down on the porch. Lane asked, "Where have you been?" He knew at once he shouldn't have asked her. He had never pried into her actions when she was younger, and she resented it now.

She frowned, anger touching her. For a moment she hesitated. Then she said, "I stopped at the store. Jess told me the Quinns came today and they're with Reardon now."

Triumph was in Lane then. He said, "You see? She's with Reardon again."

"And it's your fault. You drove Dan into making that deal with Quinn."

"My fault!" he shouted at her, outraged. "Everything is my fault. You think I want you to marry a man like Reardon? If I'd known what he was, I'd have run him out of the valley before he ever drew a month's pay from me. But I didn't know. Hiding what was in his black heart. Making love to you and all the time he was fixing to sell us out."

He knew it wasn't true, and he knew that Sue would not believe him. She rose, making no effort to hide her contempt for him.

"I'm your daughter," she said coldly. "I'll never forget that, and I'll never forget what you've done to my life."

"Damn it!" The sense of injustice grew in him. "You heard what the Quinn woman said. Haven't you got any pride?"

"Yes," she said honestly. "It was my pride that made me believe her. It made me ride over to Dan and give his ring back, and I've been sorry ever since. That was why he threw in with the Quinns. You'd told him he couldn't see me, and then I wouldn't even listen to him."

"But you can't love a man who's done what he has."

"She was lying. If I'd stopped to think, I'd have known it. He just isn't that kind."

"Oh, hell." He waved it aside with a sweep of his hand. "Women! Damned if I know how a woman thinks."

Sue walked across the porch to the door, then stopped and turned back. "No, and you don't know how a woman loves. If you did, you'd go up on the mesa and see Dan. You'd tell him there won't be any more trouble and if he wants to marry me, you'd do all you could to make us happy."

"And let him shoot me? And let Knapp go on with his horse stealing?" Lane lifted himself from his chair, cigar held tightly between his teeth. Slowly he turned, balancing his weight on his good leg. He said in a dry, tone, "I'd see you both in hell before I'd do that."

"I know. If I married Link I'd be in hell. Maybe that's what you're really driving at."

Whirling, she ran into the house. He stood staring after her until the quick, sharp sound of her heels died on the stairs. For just a moment doubts of Link Bellew washed through him. Bellew had failed the day Reardon had brought the herd into the valley; he had failed in the night attack Lane had ordered. There were times when he wondered if Bellew wanted Reardon to deliver his cattle in Gold Cup, or if Bellew was afraid of Reardon. He kept saying there was nothing he could do, that Reardon had a guard on the rim and there was no chance to get on top without losing every man Broken Bell had.

Now the Quinns were here, and Bellew had lost another chance. He could have taken the Quinns and forced a deal with Reardon. Then the doubts faded. He had to trust Bellew. He had never been wrong in his judgment of a man. He could not be wrong in Link Bellew.

Lane made a slow turn and grabbed at the porch railing, his eyes again on the rim. Anger and a sense of injury ruled him. Sue had pointed the way whereby he could save himself with her, but it was something he could not do, for the capacity to forget and forgive was not in him. Then, with striking insight, he knew that the day would come when Dan Reardon would be a bigger man than he had ever been, and rage burned like a fever in him.

He laid his great voice against the hot still air. "Damn you, Reardon! Damn you to hell!"

❧ CHAPTER 13 ❧

I T was October, with the aspens turned to orange and the scrub oak as red as flame, when Reardon and his men gathered the cattle and brought them down off the mesa. Reardon remained on the rim, watching for Bellew and the Broken Bell hands, but there was no sign of movement in the valley.

Reardon waited until the herd was across the river, then he rode down, puzzling over this. It wasn't like Ash Lane. There could be only one answer. Bellew had salted the Broken Bell crew with men like George Price who would be loyal to him, not to Lane. Bellew, then, must be playing his own game.

Reardon stopped at Vance's store, where Collie Knapp was getting supplies. Vance straightened up after dropping a sack of flour on the porch. "Well, son, you're on your way. Better sleep light with one hand reaching for your Winchester."

"Why?"

"Ash and Sue left yesterday morning for Gold Cup. Ash aims to arrange for the sale of his beef like he always has. He was in a buggy, but Sue was riding her horse."

"Where's Bellew?"

"Bringing the beef down out of the La Sals. He's a mite late this year." Vance squinted up at the towering mountain peaks, white with the first snow. "Strikes me he might be a little too late. I've seen winter come damned early around here before a man expected it."

"Ash knows this country. What's the matter with him?"

Vance shrugged. "I dunno, but Ash has failed more this summer than in the past twenty years. You know he wouldn't be taking no buggy to Gold Cup if he didn't have the miseries so bad he couldn't get into a saddle."

"A man's sins have a way of catching up with him," Collie Knapp said.

"Ash's sins don't bother him none," Vance grunted. "You know that, Dan."

This was Jess Vance's roundabout way of telling him something again, and Reardon's temper, already short under the pressure of expectant trouble, snapped as a sudden gust of anger struck him. "Speak your piece, Jess," he said hotly. "Let's have it in the kind of language I can understand."

Vance was still staring at the mountains. "I know damned well Ash don't aim for you to get that beef to Gold Cup, but I ain't figgered how Link is in any shape to make you trouble as long as he's fetching Broken Bell cows down out of the high country."

"Damn it!" Reardon bellowed. "I want to know—"

"Oh, that." Vance raised his brows as if surprised. "I didn't figger you was much interested. Why, I guess maybe Ash's miseries comes from what Sue's had to say this summer. She figgers everything would have been different if he hadn't treated you like he done." Vance turned into the store, calling back over his shoulder, "I reckon a man's love affairs is his own business, so I ain't sticking my nose in."

Reardon mounted his buckskin without looking at Knapp and rode after the herd. He tried to freeze the thought that channeled through his mind and could not. Sue still loved him despite all that had happened. His lips tightened. He had made his bargain. There could be no turning back.

They were long weary days that followed. Plodding miles that seemed to stretch on into eternity, the craggy San Juan range far ahead, the La Sals behind. Dust rising from two thousand hoofs lay upon the windless earth so that each lungful of breath was an effort and seemed the last a man could take. It was hot by day and cold by night, the air chilled by winter's promise.

At twilight killdeers winged over a near-by seep, calling their shrill cry. Purple dusk faded, and darkness closed in, and coyotes began calling from some distant rim. Broken sleep, and the tuneless singing of the night guard. Over all of it, never absent for an hour, was the pressing knowledge that somewhere, waiting for them, might be Link Bellew's men, fingers tight on triggers.

Slowly the miles fell behind. Out of the valley. Across a mesa dotted by cedars. Night in a narrow, rock-rimmed draw. Daylight. Another mesa and another draw, and night again. A nearly deserted country with only here and there a solitary nester battling a hostile land and slowly losing the starvation battle. Then down a narrow trail to the San Miguel River, running swiftly toward the Dolores, gray with tailings from the great mills around Gold Cup.

That night it rained, and in the morning the mountains glittered white with the fresh snow. It cleared by noon, and the moist earth steamed under a hot sun.

Two more days upstream, more plodding miles, tired men on tired horses, eyes straining for movement in the spruces and aspens above the trail, ears keening the wind for the crack of a Winchester, the snap of a slug that missed. Still it did not come.

They threw the herd across the river that night and held it in a box canyon. "We'll get in tomorrow," Reardon said, "if we don't have trouble."

No one spoke. Frisco Hall was too thoughtful, almost sullen. Even Hap Talley had lost his habitual grin. Finally Knapp said, "They won't stampede your steers tonight. I don't see how they can stop you now."

"I don't either," Reardon agreed, "but I don't understand it."

Boomer Shay stirred from where he hunkered beside the fire. He said, "Maybe you don't savvy Bellew, Dan. Frisco's told you all along he didn't have the guts for a stand-up fight."

"I savvy Ash Lane." Reardon fished tobacco and paper from his pockets. "Looks to me like Bellew had his own ideas."

Talley got up and stretched. "Wonder if that woman of yours lined up all them redheads."

"She will as soon as she knows we're in town."

"She'll soon know. I aim to cut my wolf loose tomorrow night." Talley licked his lips. "I'm so dry I can't even spit no more."

"You ain't drinking enough tomorrow night to work up a good spit," Hall said sharply. "Don't you forget that."

"Aw, hell," Talley groaned. "What do you think we carne up here for?"

"The ride," Hall said sarcastically.

"I aim to stand for the drinks," Reardon said. "That's the least I can do for you boys."

"No drinking." Hall glowered at Reardon. "Get that, Dan?"

Hall's green eyes narrowed. He had about him the same truculent air Reardon had noticed the day he had surprised the outlaw in Knapp's cabin. There was reason for it then, but there seemed none now. Reardon said mildly, "Sure, Frisco."

Once near morning, Reardon came awake with the thunder of a horse's hoofs on the road. He sat up, reaching for his Winchester, but the horse went on. He lay back, staring at the sky through the cottonwood limbs, wondering about it. There was little need for fast night travel in a country as thinly settled as this.

They were on the move again at dawn, pushing the cattle faster than they had in previous days, steadily eastward up the steep-walled San Miguel canyon. Reardon put Hall ahead of the herd with instructions to look out for an ambush, and he remained behind, watching the road and listening for the warning beat of hoofs. Still their luck held. It was not yet dark when they reached the corrals below Gold Cup that Quinn had built that summer.

Quinn, finishing the count, called, "Five hundred four I make it. That right, Dan?"

"That's my figger. Twenty of them are mine."

"I ain't forgot I told you we'd pay you for what was yours. Come in first thing in the morning and we'll settle up. Say, Ash Lane's in town and he's about ready to shoot himself." Quinn laughed. "He's done his damnedest, but he ain't sold a steer."

Reardon busied himself rolling a smoke. For ten years Broken Bell had furnished beef for the mining camp. Many of the butchers in Gold Cup had depended on him, and he had depended on them, and the price had always been far higher than he'd have received if he had shipped to the Denver market. Now Reardon could guess how Ash Lane felt.

Quinn was still laughing. "I told you I'd have Lane out of Long Tom Valley before spring, and I will. I hold a couple of his notes that are due in a week or so, and like-wise a mortgage. The interest is due on that. Unless I miss my guess, he'll have a hell of a time paying off."

Reardon turned away. There was no need of this, but it was Quinn's way and it was what Quinn had planned from the first. The banker called, "You're coming up tonight, ain't you?"

"Not tonight."

"Hell, Astha's expecting you."

"I ain't fit to call on a dog, Pat. I'll see her tomorrow when I'm cleaned up."

Reardon rode on then, leaving Quinn staring after him. There would be, Reardon had figured, something around seven thousand due him, the biggest stake he had ever had, and he had helped break Ash Lane to do it. Regret was a sour taste in his mouth. It had been Lane's own fault, yet there was no feeling of victory in Reardon. Lane was an old man near the end of his trail; he was a part of Long Tom Valley the same as the great cliffs that walled it.

Reardon caught up his crew, saying, "Let's have supper."

"We'll eat alone," Hall said truculently.

"What the hell." Reardon looked at him, surprised. "I was good enough to eat with you all summer."

"That ain't the proposition," Hall said. "I'm just cutting it off. That's all. We've kept our part of the bargain. You covered up for us, and we got what we wanted out of it."

"Yeah, but—"

"Let it go at that," Hall said with unnecessary violence. "You're on one side of what some damned fools call the law. We're on the other. I found out a long time ago you can't keep your feet on both sides."

It made no sense to Reardon, but he held his silence, wondering about it. Collie Knapp was riding stiffly in his saddle, staring ahead at the lights of the town, saying nothing. Something was wrong. Suddenly an invisible wall had risen between Dan Reardon and these men.

They reached Main Street, the brawling, turbulent mining camp sprawled out before them. Kerosene flares threw a smoky, flickering light into the street; barkers were already shouting their spiels before the saloons and gambling-halls. The plank walks were crowded with miners, prospectors, and freighters, elbowing and jostling and cursing amiably as they set out on the nightly search of pleasure.

Reardon turned into a livery stable, the others following, and when they walked along the runway and into the street, Hall said curtly, "So long, Dan," and moved away. Denboe and Shay followed, nodding at Reardon. Talley lingered and held out a hand. "I had a hell of a good time this summer, Dan. Maybe I'll see you again if my luck don't run out."

Reardon gripped his hand, studying Talley's youthful face that was suddenly tight and drawn in a way he had never seen it. Fear, Reardon thought, and he wondered about it. They knew, or they should know, that he wouldn't inform the local marshal. They were not wanted in Colorado, and it wasn't his business to see that they answered to Wyoming for a crime they had committed months before.

"What the hell's wrong, Hap?" Reardon asked.

"Nothing," Talley answered. "We've come to where the trail forks. That's all." He shot a quick glance at Hall's broad back. "You settling up with Quinn first thing in the morning?"

"Yeah. Why?"

"Just an idea. I don't trust bankers."

Talley wheeled and caught up with the others. Only Collie Knapp was there then, shivering a little as a gust of wind rushed down the street from the high peaks that lay around the camp.

"You'd think I was poison all of a sudden," Reardon said heavily.

"No," Knapp said. "They just want to cut their ties, Dan. I don't understand them, but then I don't understand a lot of men who live in this damned country. Maybe it's like turning a wild animal loose in town. They just don't feel comfortable."

"Well, let's eat," Reardon said. "I'm gonna get me a steak as long as your arm and then a pie. Not that your cooking wasn't all right. I just hanker for restaurant grub."

Knapp laughed, the first time Reardon had heard him laugh that day. "I'm with you, Dan. If I never see a Dutch oven again, it'll be all right with me."

They slanted across the street, boots stirring the deep dust that had been worked up by the endless procession of teams and burros and ore wagons. Finding a restaurant, they sat down at the counter and gave their orders. Reardon tapped his fingers nervously, trying not to think and failing. The quiet summer was behind, a good summer that would live long in his memory. He had liked Talley and Shay and Denboe; he had got along with Hall. He had considered them friends, but plainly they looked upon him in a different light.

"Denboe and Shay will go along with anything Hall does," Reardon said suddenly, "but Talley's different. He ain't much more'n a kid. I'd like to get him away from the rest."

"You'd better forget it," Knapp said. "You can't stop a river once it starts downhill. That's the way it is with Hap. He's set his course."

"And he's heading for a bullet in his guts or a rope on his neck," Reardon muttered. "I figger you're wrong, Collie. A man's supposed to have a brain. If he goes along downhill like a river, I say he ain't much man."

Knapp turned his head to look at him, his sensitive face holding the same drawn look that had marked Hap Talley. He said, so softly that Reardon barely heard, "I guess that's right, Dan. Not much of a man."

Their steaks came then, and Reardon covered his with ketchup and set to work. Later he had two slabs of apple pie, another cup of coffee, and drifted back into the street, Knapp beside him. They stood on the plank walk for a time, watching the milling crowd.

"Collie," Reardon said finally, "I feel like getting good and drunk, and kicking up a hell of a fight."

"No." Knapp gripped his arm tightly. "You'll need a clear head tomorrow."

"What the hell is going on?" Reardon demanded irritably. "Looks like everybody knows something but me."

Knapp dropped his hand and looked away. "You aren't as blind as you're letting on. I don't claim to be a prophet, but there's bound to be trouble before we get out of town."

Reardon thought of Ash Lane, of the rider who had gone by the camp in such a hurry, and wondered if it could have been Link Bellew. "Might be," he admitted. "Well, let's have a drink."

Later, when he was in bed, Reardon lay staring into the darkness, the brawling racket from the street beating against his ears, but they were sounds that were barely heard. He thought of Pat Quinn and Ash Lane. Then of Astha, and he wondered what she'd say because he hadn't come to see her. She'd be angry and maybe she had a right to be. If it had been Sue, he would have gone.

Then an aching sickness came to him, for he knew he had been the biggest fool a man could be, jumping into a deal he had never really believed in. At the time his reasons had been good, or they had seemed good, but now he knew they weren't. No reason was good enough to make a man marry a woman he did not love. Now he forced himself to admit something he had long known and refused to accept. He did not and he never would love Astha in the way he loved Sue Lane.

❧ CHAPTER 14 ❧

IT was the first time Dan Reardon had slept in a bed since he had left his cabin. He did not sleep well. Despite the open window, the air seemed still and stagnant. He woke at dawn from old habit, rose, and dressed. He smoked a cigarette, standing at the window and staring down into the street, now deserted and silent, pale silver in the thin light.

Slowly the town stirred sleepily to life. An old man came out of the Golden Palace, threw a bucket of dirty water into the street, and went back for another, its water as dirty as the first. A prospector appeared with his burro, heading for the high country beyond the camp. Someone behind a restaurant across the street was chopping wood, the strokes of the ax clear and metallic in the thin, chill air.

Reardon knew he should shave, felt of the week-old stubble on his face, and decided he'd stop at a barbershop before he went to the Quinn house. Then the sourness of the evening before was in him again. Astha would be waiting, probably angry, but it was mostly the prospect of going into the ornate, costly house that went against his grain. He did not belong there. He never would.

He went out, pausing outside Knapp's door. He heard no sound. Collie Knapp had been able to sleep in a bed better than he had. He went down the deserted hall, descended the stairs, and crossed to the restaurant where he had eaten with Knapp the evening before. By the time he had finished breakfast, the sun was showing above the mountain ridges to the east, and people were on the street. He lingered in front of the restaurant, reaching for tobacco and paper, and immediately dropped his hand. Sue Lane was coming down the walk toward him.

He had not seen her since she had thrown his ring at him and ridden out of his yard. Now he stood motionless, pulling in short quick breaths, feeling his desire for her in every nerve and muscle. Apparently she was not aware of his presence until she was within ten feet of him. Then she saw him. She stopped suddenly, color washing out of her cheeks.

Reardon took off his hat, asking hoarsely, "How are you, Sue?"

She had the look of a bird about to take flight, and for an instant he thought she was going to run past him without speaking. Her hands fisted at her sides, and opened, and some of the stiffness went out of her. "I'm fine, Dan. How are you?"

She was thinner than he had ever seen her, and there were lines around her eyes that were new. She was wearing a long-sleeved blue dress, one that she had bought since she had come to Gold Cup, he thought, for he had not seen it before.

"I'm all right." He looked down at his worn shirt that should be patched, suddenly conscious of his need for a shave and a haircut. "Just got in last night. Haven't had time to get cleaned up."

She stood motionless, breathing hard. Her chestnut hair was aflame with the sharp morning sun upon it. Now, facing her unexpectedly this way, he found himself more deeply stirred by her presence than he had ever been before. He reached for the makings, his hands trembling so that he spilled more tobacco than he dribbled into the curled paper. He thought, *Hold on, Reardon. Don't let her see how you feel.*

"Dan," she said, "don't stay in town. Dad's here. I guess you know you've broken him."

Sealing the cigarette, he said, "That's something I didn't aim to do."

"You'll never make Dad believe that. If he sees you, he'll pull his gun, and you'd kill him. You could draw ten guns in the time it would take him to pull. His rheumatism has been awfully bad this summer."

He looked at her, saw her lips tremble, and in that moment he hated both himself and Pat Quinn. "I wouldn't kill Ash," he said. "You know that."

"If you didn't, he'd kill you. That's the way he feels." She bit her lower lip, fighting for self-control. Then she said, "You don't know how it is to lose everything you've given your life to build."

If Ash Lane hadn't been so bullheaded and selfish, he wouldn't be losing anything now. Sue knew that, but Reardon could not remind her of it. He said, "No, I don't know, seeing as I never had anything myself."

"If you don't have now," she flung at him scornfully, "you will. You're the partner of the great Patrick Quinn, and in ten years you'll be just like him." She bowed her head, blinking hard. "That's what hurts, Dan. Whatever

Dad is or has been, he's a saint alongside Quinn."

"I don't guess Pat's quite that bad," Reardon said.

"You don't think so." She raised her head and looked squarely at him. "Ask him what happened to the butchers who refused to take his orders. The talk around here is that he murdered three men to control the market."

She swept past him then, head held high. He watched her until she disappeared into the Conner House, his thoughts on Quinn. What she said might be true, but he found it hard to believe. Turning, he went on to the bank. Quinn was inside, and when he heard Reardon rattle the door, he came out of his private office in the back and opened the front door.

"A little early, ain't you, Dan?" he asked crustily.

"Maybe. Just saw Sue Lane. She says Ash is blaming me. I don't want trouble with him, Pat."

Quinn led the way back to his office, Reardon following. He sat down and drew his swivel chair up to the mahogany desk. "No, I reckon you wouldn't. You pulling out before you see Astha?"

Reardon shook his head. "I'll get some decent clothes and go up to the house. Then I'll slope out." He threw his money belt down on the desk. "There's a little over three thousand left from your check I cashed in Moab."

Quinn removed the money and counted it. Then he leaned back and said challengingly, "Astha's figgering on getting married right away."

"Any day she sets, but I aim to stay clear of Ash." He dug a worn sheet of paper from his pocket and laid it on the desk. "There's the figgers on what I spent for the cattle and supplies."

Quinn looked at it, reached for a pad of paper, and figured for several minutes. Without glancing up, he said,
"Your twenty head are worth two thousand. Now the way
this looks, you've got another fifty-five hundred coming.
That what you get?"

"Suits me."

Quinn rose, took the money from the safe, and gave it
to Reardon. He said, "It was a good summer for both of
us. Now there's no sense of you going back to the valley.
Too much danger for Astha. I'll stake you to a honeymoon
in Denver. In the spring Lane will be gone. We'll use
Broken Bell—"

Reardon leaned forward, hands palm down on the
desk. "Look, Pat. I told Astha I wasn't going along with
you. Didn't she tell you?"

For a moment Quinn's face was blank. Then he said
softly, "Well, I'll be damned. No, she didn't tell me anything. What the hell's the matter with you?"

"I just don't play your way. Sue said the talk was you'd
murdered three butchers who wouldn't line up with you.
I don't want any part of it."

The banker laughed. "So that's it. She's lying, boy. I
had to be a little rough on three of them, all right. One shot
himself. The other two sloped out of camp. That's as far
as I went."

"It doesn't make any difference. I don't play your
way."

Quinn scratched a smoothly-shaven chin. "You know,
of course, I wouldn't have made my offer in the first place
if I hadn't thought it would work into a permanent partnership. I need you to handle this cattle project, and you

need me. I know how Astha spends money."

"If she loves me," Reardon said harshly, "she'll live my way. If she don't, it's a hell of a mistake for us to get married."

"Now that might be," Quinn agreed. "I tell you what you do, Dan. Go up and see her. Talk it over. We'll let it stand that way."

Reardon put his money in his belt and buckled it around him. "You can let it stand any way you want to, but I know what I'm going to do." Wheeling, he left the bank.

There was still the meeting with Astha. Reardon thought about it as he bought a new shirt and a pair of Levis, and walked back to the hotel. He climbed the stairs, wondering what he would say to her. If she loved him, she would live his way. But was a man ever sure a woman loved him? And how could he tell her he loved her when he could not put Sue out of his mind?

He moved along the hall toward his room, and as he passed Knapp's door, he heard Hall's voice, harsh and commanding "Collie, I won't take no for an answer. You've got the same smell on you we've got, and there's no sense pretending different. Now you'll be in on this job, or, by hell, you won't be alive when I leave town."

"Go ahead," Knapp shouted. "Kill me. I guess I don't really care."

Reardon dropped his package and, opening Knapp's door, slid in. Hall was standing by the window, so angry he was trembling. Denboe and Shay were on the bed. Talley slumped in a chair across the room. Knapp stood beside the door, his face as white as a dead man's.

"Get out," Hall said thickly. "We finished with you last night. From here on it's my show."

"Sounded like maybe it was my show," Reardon said.

"I've taken your last order," Hall bellowed. "Now you're taking mine if you want to live. Get out."

Reardon heeled the door shut behind him. "I'm dealing myself in, Frisco. What's this about not taking no for an answer?"

"They're holding up the bank at noon," Knapp said in a low tone. "They want me in. I'm on the wrong side of the law, too, Dan, but I refuse to rob a bank. Even when it belongs to Pat Quinn."

There was silence, a tight, pregnant silence that ran out into seconds while shock held Dan Reardon motionless. A lot of things were explained. Hap Talley's question the night before about when Reardon was settling up with Quinn. The way they had cut him off after they'd reached camp, wanting to be alone. And it explained what Frisco Hall had planned from the first. It was not so much the hide-out in a cow camp as it was the fact that, having worked for an outfit partly owned by Quinn, they had a legitimate excuse for being in Gold Cup and no suspicion would fall upon them before the holdup.

Suddenly Hall laughed, a grating sound that reached across the room and jarred Reardon. Hall said, "You played hell telling Dan, Collie. We didn't want trouble with him."

"You won't have trouble," Knapp said in a tone pulled thin by fear.

Then Reardon found his voice. "He'll have a hell of a lot of trouble if he pulls this job off. I'm responsible for you being here, Frisco, and I'm damned if I'm going to let you rob a bank."

Hall shrugged. "That's what I was getting at, Collie. Quinn'll be his daddy-in-law, and Quinn ain't gonna like it when he figgers out how it worked. Might even get the notion that Dan fetched us up here for a split."

"I'm telling you," Reardon raged. "You hold up that bank and I'll hunt you to hellangone."

Hall laughed again, the same jarring sound. "You're asking for a slug in your belly, son." He pinned his sharp green eyes on Knapp. "Like I was saying, Collie. We need you for this job. They've got a tough hand for a marshal. One of them gents who rides a horse up and down the street looking mean as all hell so nobody'll step out of line. He always eats dinner at noon across from the bank. We need a man to keep him inside. Another man to manage the horses. That'll be you. Three of us will take care of the job inside."

"You don't really need me," Knapp cried.

"Figger it any way you want to," Hall said harshly, "but that's the way it's gonna be. Maybe I don't really trust you, Collie. You know a hell of a lot about us."

Knapp looked at Reardon, his eyes begging. "That's their real reason, Dan."

Now Reardon saw the depth of Collie Knapp's weakness. He was a thin character without any solid courage, the kind of man who went downstream with whatever current seized him. Last night he had been talking about himself, not Hap Talley. Now he was trying to hold to one last belief, but in the end he would go if left to himself.

Hall stood motionless by the window, a wide, massive

man, unbending, solid in his determination to bend others to his desires. Shay and Denboe rose from the bed and waited for the break. They had long ago been shaped by Hall's will; they would back him now regardless of their own feelings. But Hap Talley was something else. He rose, lazily and quite casually, and moved toward Reardon, eyes on Hall.

"Don't try it, Frisco," Talley said. "I ain't like Monte and Boomer. I still do my own thinking."

"Meaning what?" Hall demanded.

"Meaning that you're figgering on smoking Dan down. If you do, you'd better smoke me, too."

"I guess we could do that," Hall flung at him. "Have you gone off your nut, Hap? You know what I do to men who buck me."

"And you know I'm fast enough to get Boomer or Monte," Talley said coolly, "and I've got a hunch Dan's fast enough to take you."

Hall stood thinking it over. Knapp could be counted out, but Talley could not. So the odds were three to two instead of four to one as he had been figuring.

It was Reardon who laughed then. "Looks like you missed your guess with Hap, Frisco. He ain't your kind."

"You're making a mistake, Hap," Hall said softly.

"Maybe. Either way, there's some things a man can do and some he can't. Standing around while a man gets smoked down who's been as straight with us as Dan has is something I can't do."

"Ain't you a little ahead of me?" Hall asked. "Who said anything about smoking Dan down?"

"I can read that ugly mug of yours like a book," Talley

said scornfully. "You figgered you had to drill him the minute he came in."

"You'll have that tough marshal after you if you start shooting," Knapp cried in his high, thin voice. "What'll happen to your holdup plan, then?"

"Now that's real sharp thinking," Hall said, his tone suddenly amiable. "That's why I want you with us. We can use a brain like you've got. All right, Hap. Get down off your high horse. We don't bother your friend Dan, but what I said about Collie goes. We're walking into the bank at five minutes after twelve. Hap takes care of the marshal. Collie, you be in front of the bank at twelve. We'll have five horses and you're riding with us."

There would be no shooting trouble now. Reardon knew that, but he knew, too, that Hall was masking his real intent with a quick show of giving way. He said, "Frisco, take your boys and ride out of town. I won't let you hold up that bank."

"You'll have a hell of a time stopping us," Hall said easily. He jerked his head at the door. "Come on. We've got a few chores to attend to."

Reardon watched them go out, Talley pulling the door shut behind him. He waited, hearing their steps die along the hall. He looked at his watch. Ten o'clock. Still plenty of time. He said, "Stay here, Collie. I'll find the marshal."

Reardon opened the door but he did not leave the room. Boomer Shay stood outside, his gun in his hand. He said flatly, "The minute you step out here, you're a dead man." Reardon looked at Shay's knobby, wicked face, and went back into the room and closed the door.

CHAPTER 15

QUICKLY Reardon crossed the room and, opening the window, looked down into the alley that lay beside the hotel. It was a long drop to the ground, and this was no time to risk a broken leg. He crossed the room to the bed, jerked up the sheets, and knotted them together.

"Hang on to one end, Collie," Reardon said. "I'm going down."

"They'll kill you, Dan," Knapp breathed. "Don't do it. We'll stay here. They won't come back after me."

"My hide's tough," Reardon said.

He moved back to the window. Then he swore bitterly and dropped the sheets. Monte Denboe stood in the street end of the alley, eyes on the window. Reardon drew his gun and let it slide back. He couldn't shoot Denboe like this.

Reardon crossed the room and dropped into a chair. "They've got us between a rock and a hard place," he said. "We'll wait a while."

Knapp sat on the bed, eyes on the floor. "I told you once I had achieved a kind of peace I had never known, Dan, but it was a false peace. I knew it could not last. Your way of meeting a problem head on when it comes is the only way."

"I guess there's some things I don't savvy."

"You will," Knapp groaned, "and you'll hate me. I told you when Lane started it last spring that I wasn't worth anything." He raised his head and looked at Reardon, aching misery stamped upon his face. "I started running from myself a long time ago and I never stopped. I grew up with more advantages than most men had. A good home and all the money I needed. I had an education. I could have worked in my dad's store, been respectable, got married, had kids. I threw it away for a woman like Astha. I think of her every time I see Astha. Telling me one thing when all the time she really wanted something else."

Knapp waved it away. "No use going into that. I robbed my dad's safe so I could buy her the things I thought she should have, but when the blue chip was down, she wouldn't go with me. I left home. Drifted until I got here. I never had the courage to go back and face it."

"Was that what Hall meant when he said you had the same smell they had?"

"He didn't know about that." Knapp clenched his fists and dropped his gaze to the floor again. "This is another case of running away. I didn't have the courage to tell you, Dan. I couldn't take the chance of driving away the one honest man who believed in me."

"You weren't working with the horse thieves—"

"No. I didn't lie to you, Dan. It was Bellew who was in with the horse thieves. He built the signal fires to tell them it was all right to come on. He always worked it so that the Broken Bell crew was not at the place where the horses crossed the river."

"You sure of that?" Reardon asked.

"I'm sure, but what would my word count in Long Tom Valley against a man Ash Lane trusted?" Knapp shook his head. "I couldn't do anything. My hands were tied because Bellew knew what I was doing. I gave a hide-out to any outlaw who came through. Guided him to the Hole. Brought him supplies. Warned him if it was necessary. It paid me well enough until Bellew got onto it. Then he started blackmailing me. I've been paying him half of what I got, and he agreed to hold Lane off. I've wondered about that time you stopped them on the rim. Maybe Bellew decided to shut my mouth for good."

"Hell, if he was with the horse thieves, you could have—"

Knapp rose and walked to the window. "Look at it honestly, Dan. Anybody in the valley would believe Bellew because of Ash Lane, but nobody would believe me. They condemned me from the first. That's the way people are. Honest and smug as hell, but they run in a pack like horse thieves or bank robbers. So I paid to protect myself and my business. All I could do was hope that Bellew would keep his word."

"Hall and the others knew Bellew?"

Knapp nodded. "Actually he was hiding out in the valley as much as Hall and his bunch were hiding out in the Hole, but his protection was Lane's belief in him. Hall says he's wanted in Montana for cattle rustling. Outlaws have their standards to live by the same as honest people, and Bellew was a crook by those standards. I don't know the details, but he sent his partners to prison so he could have their money as well as his. Some way he got word to the sheriff where the others were hiding out."

"That time I met Bellew on the trail—" Reardon began.

"He'd been up to collect half of what Hall's bunch had

paid me. Now he's demanding five thousand dollars. He says he'll get out of the country if I pay him, but I haven't got it."

"You mean Bellew's here in town? Now?"

"He's here all right. Passed us night before last. I don't know what he's up to, but he must be planning to make a big haul of some kind. He's been playing for the big pot."

"Meaning what?"

"Sue, thinking he'll have Broken Bell when Ash dies. Now he's made his mind he can't get her, and he's planning to clean up all he can. I don't know, but I think that some of the new men he's brought to Broken Bell like George Price are part of the horse-thief bunch."

Reardon's mind was racing ahead of Knapp. Ash Lane would not believe what Knapp had to say, but Sue might, and if she did, there was a chance she could make her father listen. A big haul could mean only one thing—the Broken Bell herd that Bellew was supposed to be starting for Gold Cup.

Knapp stood at the window, staring across the narrow valley at the bald, granite-topped peak to the south. Now, without turning, he said, his tone bitter with self-mockery, "I've given you a lot of empty words about not caring what happened to me, but they were lies, the only lies I've ever told you. I'm afraid to die, and I'm afraid to go to prison. If I don't give that money to Bellew, he'll tell the sheriff what he knows."

"He's bluffing you, Collie. With his record, he couldn't take a chance on stirring up a sheriff. Quit worrying about him. I want you—"

Still staring across the valley, Knapp said, "The Lord

gave me the body of a man. I wish to hell I could die like one."

"Collie, I want you—"

Knapp swung around to face Reardon, a muscle in his cheek twitching with the regularity of a pulse beat. "Dan, I'm going to get a gun and shoot Bellew. That's the only way. It would be the greatest thing I ever did."

Only then did Reardon sense how far the long-suppressed fear and self-condemnation had taken Collie Knapp. Reardon rose and, coming to Knapp, laid a hand on his shoulder. "Collie, forget that. Leave the fighting to me."

"Sure. That's what I've always done. I did it the night Bellew made his attack when we were in your cabin, but I can't keep on. I've got to quit looking like a man or start acting like one."

"You're no good to anybody dead, but you're mighty important alive. Look, Collie. Shay won't let me out of here, but he won't keep you."

"Yes, I suppose he'll let me go. I'll get a gun—"

Reardon said, "Shut that up," and slapped him across the face.

The man cringed away from him, trembling, and then he regained his composure. "All right, Dan. What is it you want me to do?"

"Go to the Conner House and get Sue. Bring her here. I want you to tell her what you've told me."

"About me giving a hide-out—"

"About Bellew and the horse thieves."

Knapp stood motionless, his head lowered, the old fears washing through him again. "I don't want to see Lane."

"Don't see him. Ask for Sue at the desk. Tell her anything you want to, but get her over here." Reardon looked at his watch. "It ain't half past ten yet. Plenty of time to stop Hall."

Reardon opened the door. Shay had pulled up a chair and was sitting directly across the hall. He grinned at Reardon. "I'm still here and you're still there. That's the way it's staying."

"Sure. I never auger with Mr. Colt. It's Collie who wants to leave."

Shay's eyes narrowed. "Well, I dunno about that. What for, Collie?"

"I'm going after Sue Lane. Dan wants her."

Shay's grin returned. That was something he could understand. "I reckon that would be all right. Frisco didn't say anything about women. But don't make a mistake, Collie, and go after that marshal, or your pal's a dead man."

"I don't want to see a marshal," Collie said, and darted down the hall.

Reardon shut the door. It might not work. He could hope. Nothing more. He walked to the window. Denboe was still in the alley. Reardon smoked a cigarette, the waiting bringing a tension in him. Suddenly he laughed aloud. Six months ago he would have said to hell with Lane. When a man dug his own grave and jumped into it, he might as well stay there. Even now he knew that it was not Ash Lane who was making him do this. It was Sue. She had said that in ten years he'd be like Pat Quinn. He had to show her that wasn't true.

A tap on the door brought him around. He hesitated,

thinking that if it was Knapp, he wouldn't knock. He laid a hand on gun butt, calling, "Come in."

The door swung open. Sue stood there, hesitating. "Knapp said—"

"Where is he?"

"He left me in the lobby. Said you wanted to see me."

It was Reardon who hesitated then, not liking it. Boomer Shay called, "Let her in, boy. If a purty gal came to my hotel room, I'd be damned if I'd keep her waiting in the hall."

"Shut up, Boomer. Come in, Sue." Slowly she stepped inside and Reardon closed the door behind her. "I knew Ash wouldn't come, and he wouldn't believe Collie if he did. That's why I sent for you. Now that Collie isn't here, you'll have to believe me."

He motioned toward the one chair in the room and dropped down on the unmade bed. For a moment he looked at her, thinking that this summer had added years to her life. She met his gaze, waiting to hear what he had to say. Six months ago she would have been bubbling with impatience. Now she sat motionless, fingers laced together on her lap.

"Bellew's in town, ain't he?" Reardon asked.

She nodded. "He's at the Conner House."

"Did he say why he came?"

"The herd's on its way. He came on ahead to see if Dad had sold it."

"Was that necessary?"

"No," she said. "Dad didn't like it. Link belongs with the herd. Selling was Dad's job."

"I'll tell you the real reason he came. He's leaving the

country, and he's got some kind of a big scheme cooked up to fill his pockets. He came up here before he left to shake Collie down for five thousand dollars."

He had half expected her to jump up and scream that it was a lie, but she didn't. She sat without moving, her fingers still laced. She said evenly, "How could he shake Knapp down for that much money?"

Reardon told her the story Knapp had told him about Bellew's background. Then he told the rest of it, about what Knapp had been doing and who Hall's bunch was. He added, "I didn't want to tell you the whole yarn, but there wasn't no quitting place. You can think what you want to, but I'd hate to see Ash go under. That's why I'm telling all of it. You've got to make Ash believe what Bellew is."

She rose and walked to the window, her head held high. "Why did you tell me this, Dan?"

"I told you. Ash will be in bad shape if he loses that herd."

"He'll be broke," she said tonelessly. "If he didn't lose it, and shipped to Denver, it would be too late. He couldn't get his money in time to pay Quinn."

"Maybe I can help him."

"After all that's happened, are you trying to tell me you're so fond of Dad that you want to save his hide? Or are you taking this way to get at Link?"

"I'll handle Link when the sign's right," he said with sudden anger.

She put a hand to her forehead as if it had begun to ache. "I think Link was loyal to Broken Bell as long as he thought he would eventually marry me, but he finally got it through his head he never would. What you said about him letting the stolen horses through the valley makes sense. He always had an excuse for failing to catch them just as he always had an excuse for not stopping you this summer. I suppose that he didn't really care whether you came up here or not. Perhaps he was planning on stealing our trail herd all the time."

"Then get over to Ash and tell him what I've told you."

"If I do, he'll go to the sheriff and have Knapp and your trail crew arrested."

For the moment Reardon had forgotten the holdup. He jerked out his watch. It was ten minutes after eleven. He said, "Then don't tell him all of it. Just tell him enough so he'll fire Link."

"Now you're talking crazy. It doesn't make much sense unless you know it all."

"You've got to try."

She swung away from the window and laid her gaze directly upon his face. "I don't think you've told me the real reason you want to save Dad."

He got up from the bed and crossed the room to her. "All right. I haven't. I keep thinking about what you said this morning. About me being like Pat Quinn. I'm not and I never will be, but I suppose you won't believe me any more than you did that morning when you rode over and asked if Astha had been there the night before. You wouldn't even listen."

"Was she?"

"She was there," he said hoarsely, "but I slept in the barn."

A small smile touched the corners of her mouth. "Dan,

you'll never know how many times I've cried myself to sleep and hated myself for not listening that morning. I've blamed Dad, but when I'm really honest with myself, I know it's been my fault as much as his."

She wanted him; she was waiting, begging with her eyes. He stepped back, pushing her away with his will. "I made a bargain with Astha. I'll keep it."

She stared at him incredulously. "You wouldn't wreck our lives because of a promise. You aren't that big a fool, Dan."

"That's just the size fool I am."

"Why, it wouldn't even be fair to Astha."

"I think it's what she wants."

"I won't let you, Dan." She came quickly to him and put her hands on his shoulders, her face held up to his. "I've tried to hate you, but I can't. We belong together. Don't go to her."

A gun sounded in the street, and then again, raising echoes that slammed against the false fronts. Reardon's first thought was that Hall had jumped the time on the holdup. He lunged across the room, heard Sue cry, "Stay here, Dan. It's nothing to you," but he didn't stop. He jerked the door open. Shay was gone.

Reardon ran down the stairs and into the street. Then he saw it was not the holdup. Men had rushed out of stores and saloons to form a tight circle around a man in the dust. A doctor was running along the boardwalk, yelling, "Get back, get back."

Reardon laid heavy shoulders against the ring of men and battered his way through. He stopped, breath sawing out of him, and he could not, for what seemed a long moment, suck air back into his lungs. It was Collie Knapp who lay in the deep dust of the street.

❧ CHAPTER 16 ❧

REARDON dropped down on his knees beside Knapp. He was on his back, blood a scarlet froth at the corners of his mouth. His right hand was flung out beside him, a new gun a foot away. He was breathing in bubbling gasps; the knowledge of death shadowed his dark eyes.

The medico was tugging at Reardon's shoulder. "Get away. Get away. Let me look at him."

"No use, Doc," Knapp whispered, "Dan will do me more good than you can." He fought a hand up to Reardon's shoulder. "You're always there when you're needed. You're the one shining star in a long and lonely night."

Cursing, the medico came around to Knapp's left side and kneeling beside him, began to unbutton his shirt. Knapp said, "Never mind, Doc." He was smiling a little. "You know, Dan, now it's here, I'm not afraid to die. I'll find the peace that has always eluded me, but you'll find yours on this earth where I failed. Your way of meeting problems head on is the only way." His hand slid down from Reardon's shoulder and lay loose in the dust as he took a gurgling breath. It was his last.

Reardon rose, shaking under the pressure of his emotions. He looked around the circle of men, knowing none of them. A big man with a star on his flannel shirt sat his saddle in the fringe of the crowd. Reardon asked in a voice he did not know, "Who did it?"

"Link Bellew," someone said.

"It was a fair fight," another said. "I saw it. This man called to Bellew that he was going to kill him. He had his gun in his waistband. Bellew turned around and drew. He was faster."

"Knapp couldn't shoot," Reardon said in that same strange voice. "It was murder. What are you going to do about it, marshal?"

The lawman shrugged. "You heard what Matt just said, mister. It was a fair fight."

"Damn you, it was murder. I told you Knapp couldn't shoot."

The marshal smiled tolerantly. "It ain't murder in my book, friend."

Reardon started, toward him, blind in his rage. He heard the shout, "Holdup! The bank's been held up!" and was only then aware of the fading beat of running horses.

The crowd swirled away from Reardon and the marshal. They faced each other, Reardon shouting, "All right. If that's what the law is here, I'll handle Bellew myself."

"Take it easy," the marshal warned.

"Quinn's hurt," a man yelled from the bank. "Get over here, Doc."

"Wait a minute." One of the bank tellers ran up, pointing a finger at Reardon. "The men who held up the bank belonged to Reardon's crew. I was at the corral when they came in last night. He must have known about this."

"Yeah, that might be," the marshal said. "What about it?"

Reardon was close beside the marshal now, staring up

at the man's high-boned face. "Why ain't you' going after 'em?"

"That's outside of my ballywick, friend. I'd have stopped 'em if I hadn't been sucked in on this ruckus. Now it's up to the sheriff."

"The sheriff ain't in town," someone said.

"I tell you Reardon must have been in on it," the bank teller bellowed. "He fetched them outlaws to town."

The growl of the crowd beat against Reardon's ears. There would be no reasoning here. No sound logic could hold him responsible for a crime they all knew he had no part in committing, but logic was never part of a mob's reaction. They had him, the others were gone, and Pat Quinn was hurt, perhaps dying.

On impulse, Reardon reached up and tumbled the marshal out of the saddle, shouting, "I'll bring them back." Then he was in leather, and digging in the steel. The crowd broke away from in front of his horse. Someone shot at him and missed. The marshal let out a bull-like bellow of rage, and again a gun went off. Then Reardon was out of town, the wind slapping at his breath.

Hall's thinking was plain enough. It was still half an hour before the time he'd set for the holdup, but the fight in the street had attracted the crowd and the marshal, and Hall's bunch had been ready. The big black that Reardon forked was a good horse, but the outlaws' mounts were faster and they were pulling steadily ahead.

Reardon, seeing he could not overtake them in one burst of speed, pulled his black down to a slower pace. During the summer months he had learned to know these men well, and now he considered what they would do.

Hall was the acknowledged leader. He had earned and kept his position by superiority of mind and gun skill; perhaps partly, too, by his lack of conscience and complete ruthlessness once he had decided upon his objective. If it came to a showdown now, he would kill Dan Reardon as quickly as he would kill any man who attempted to stop him.

Denboe and Shay were the followers, born to take the way that was charted for them the same as Hall was born to do the charting. They had made no secret of their past to Reardon. For them there could be no turning back; they were wanted in too many places. As with Hall, friendship would end the moment Reardon tried to recover the bank's money.

Talley was the question mark. Reardon did not believe what Collie Knapp had said about a man going downstream with the current once he had set his course. That had been Knapp's way, so it was natural that he would judge Talley's reaction to be the same. On the other hand, Reardon was the kind who swam upstream, and he sensed that same capacity in young Talley. This morning Talley had stood alongside Reardon, saying he did his own thinking. That was not entirely true. Still, Reardon thought there was a good chance that at the finish he would turn against Hall. As far as Reardon knew, the kid had only one other charge against him, the U.P. robbery at Desert Wells. This job in Gold Cup would be his second.

There was little chance for Reardon if the odds stood four to one. He could expect no help from a Gold Cup posse. One would be along eventually, but with the sheriff out of town and the marshal having to stay in Gold Cup, there was little chance the posse would have adequate leadership.

So, in the long run, the future of Quinn's bank depended upon what Reardon succeeded in doing. At the same time he would be deciding his own fate. He had acted entirely upon impulse. Now that he had time to think about it, he saw that it had been a rash decision. The marshal would not think favorably on being pulled out of his saddle; he would look with less favor upon the loss of his horse.

Reardon could not even be sure how Astha and her father would consider what he had done. Quinn might decide, as someone in the crowd had said, that Dan Reardon had brought Hall's bunch to Gold Cup to rob the bank, and that he was expecting his cut from the stolen money. Quinn would be remembering Reardon had come in very early that morning to settle up, early enough, Quinn would think, to get all he had coming before the holdup. The one man who could have cleared Reardon of any part in the robbery was Collie Knapp, and Collie Knapp was dead.

Not since Reardon had been old enough to make his own decisions had he been on what he considered the wrong side. He wasn't sure that he was now, for there was little to choose between Ash Lane and Pat Quinn, and in returning the bank's money, he was strengthening the man with whom he must completely break.

Ash Lane had often said that a man's actions were determined by one of two things—fear or money. The statement was a half-truth, but it was a whole truth as far as these men were concerned who had woven the threads of life into the sorry fabric that had dropped over Dan Reardon. Lane, Quinn, the outlaws—except Hap Talley—all were driven by one or the other, or both.

It struck Reardon now that there was little real difference between Hall on one hand, and Lane and Quinn on the other. Lane and Quinn operated within the law; Hall, boldly despising the controls that the state had put upon its people, took what he wanted at the point of a gun. The age-old pattern and the age-old motives, all adding up to failure and death for Dan Reardon if he did not return Quinn's money. Then his thoughts completed the circle and came again to Hap Talley. If he sided Reardon, the odds would be three to two, and Reardon would have a chance.

There was still no indication that a posse had taken the trail. The sun was low in the west now. Another hour would bring dusk, another complete darkness. The outlaws had doubtless known that one man at least was in pursuit, and would guess who it was. There was a possibility they would try to ambush him. Again Talley was the question mark, for he was not the kind who would have any part of a bushwhack scheme.

Dust marking the outlaws' passage hung in the still air. Some of them, then, must be ahead, but Reardon had no way of knowing whether all of them were or not. It would be like Hall, unless Talley had been able to influence him, to send one of them, probably Boomer Shay, off the road to wait with a cocked Winchester in his hand. Without conscious direction, Reardon's eyes lifted to the brushy side of the canyon. Then he gave a small bitter laugh as he realized what he was doing. If one of them was waiting for him, he'd ride into the trap and be killed, for there would be no warning, and Boomer Shay was not one to miss.

Fear struck Dan Reardon then. It was different when they had driven the herd upstream. There had been six of them, enough to make a fight if Link Bellew had struck. Now he was alone. One bullet would do the job.

Taking a long breath, Reardon fought down the panic that threatened to rush over him. It was not his way to worry about something which might happen. He forced himself to consider other courses of action the outlaws could take. They would head for Knapp's Hole if the U.P. money was hidden there, and Reardon thought it was. With Collie Knapp gone, they wouldn't remain. Robbers' Roost in Utah would likely be their final objective. Once there, Reardon's chances of finding them would be less than nothing. It was a wild, barren country where a man who did not know the location of the water holes would soon be turned back.

Then a new thought struck Reardon. At the speed they were traveling, their horses would not hold up. Obviously they had planned to outdistance pursuit at this end of the trail, but they were too old hands at the game to let themselves be caught with tired mounts. Usually they had arranged for relays of fresh horses along their line of flight, but Reardon was sure they had no such arrangements this time. It was a long way to Knapp's Hole, more miles before they could expect to find fresh mounts in Utah to take them on to Robbers' Roost.

Reardon considered the possibility of their stealing horses in Long Tom Valley, and decided against it. Hall would be too smart to stir up a hornets' nest if he could avoid it, and it would be a hornets' nest, for the valley people had long been edgy over the stolen bands that had been rushed through the valley the previous spring.

Logic forced Reardon to one answer. The outlaws would make a try at Gebhardt's horses on the river. Abe Gebhardt had a ranch in the canyon below Placerville. Now that he thought about it, Reardon remembered Talley's casual remark about the good-looking bays Gebhardt had in his corrals.

Reardon was acquainted with Gebhardt, a salty old-timer who had settled on the San Miguel about the time Ash Lane had gone to Long Tom Valley. He'd make it rough on Hall's bunch if he had an opportunity, but whether he'd have the opportunity was a question. Hall would be desperate, but hardly desperate enough to murder a man for his horses. Monte Denboe had once said with pride that most of their jobs had been bloodless ones because Hall insisted a killing always aroused a wild fury that mere robbery never produced.

Half a mile above Placerville, Reardon crossed the river to avoid riding through the settlement. It was what Hall would do, so Reardon would learn nothing in the town, and he might run into trouble. Hall, in his careful way, had doubtless cut the telegraph wires below Gold Cup, perhaps sending a man to do the job before the bank had been robbed. If, on the other hand, the wires had not been cut, or if the line had been repaired, the Placerville marshal would be watching for Reardon as well as Hall's bunch.

Fording the murky stream below town, Reardon came

back into the road and brought his horse to a faster pace. Half an hour later he saw Gebhardt's buildings and swung into the brush, knowing this was his only chance. If he had guessed wrong, the pursuit would run on for miles and probably end in failure.

There was a fringe of willows along the river, and Reardon left his black there. He stood watching the clearing for a long moment. The light was very thin now. Apparently the place was deserted, but there were horses in the corrals.

Keeping low, Reardon made a run for the cabin. He reached the blank back wall and dropped flat, his heart hammering in great sledgelike beats in his chest. Dan Reardon had never been afraid of a fight in his life, but this was like hunting a shadow. He wormed his way around the corner of the cabin, watching the corrals. Five horses were bunched behind the barn, more beyond them.

There was no indication that the outlaws were here. Doubts began to plague Reardon. Hall's bunch had been ahead of him all the way down from Gold Cup. It was possible they had bought the horses and gone on. Or they might be waiting until it was fully dark before moving in if they aimed to steal the bays. A hazy gray light still lingered along the horizon. It would be another half hour before it faded completely.

Gebhardt, Reardon thought, must be gone. Otherwise he would have the lamp going. He owned a small outfit, raising his own hay here along the river and never letting his horses get any farther away than the pasture back of the barn. On the other hand, if he was gone, Hall would have made his try for the horses before now.

Reardon pondered it and came to no conclusion. Then he heard the beat of horses' hoofs on the road, and a band of riders swept by. The posse, Reardon judged, and smiled tolerantly. They'd have the ride. Nothing more.

He bellied on around to the front of the cabin, keeping below the one window. He called softly, "Gebhardt."

"Come on in, Dan," Talley said.

Reardon's first impulse was to get up and walk in. He came as far as his hands and knees and stayed that way for a moment, a faint chill of warning sliding down his back. This was too easy.

"Might be better if you came out, Hap," Reardon said.

"Why," Talley said easily, "you've got no reason not to trust me. Or maybe you forgot I sided you this morning in Collie's room."

"No, I ain't forgot."

"Well, come on in."

A man's character was a treacherous thing on which to gamble a life. Reardon would make that gamble on Hap Talley's loyalty as soon as any man's, and sooner than most. Still, it was a gamble, and there was more than Dan Reardon's life at stake.

"I don't like the smell of it, Hap," Reardon said. "Too damned quiet around here."

"We ain't real noisy," Talley said.

"Who's with you?"

"Gebhardt, but he ain't feeling sociable. We came in 'bout an hour ago and wanted a meal and some horses. He cooked up the meal, then he got stubborn when it came to selling us the horses. Claimed he didn't have nothing but breeding stock, and was going after his gun to show he meant business, so Frisco tapped him on the head."

"Dead?"

"Hell, no. He's just taking a nap. Now come in with your hands up. I ain't fixing to throw no lead your direction, and I don't want any coming mine."

It had probably happened the way Talley said, but Reardon wasn't sure about the lead throwing. He asked, "Where's the rest of 'em?"

"In the barn. They've got saddles on four of Gebhardt's horses. Soon as we get you tied up, we'll be on our way."

"What makes you think I'll walk in so you can put a rope on me?"

"Because you're smart. If you don't, you'll get a slug in your brisket. Look, Dan. The other three are in the barn. I'm here. That's four guns to your one. Frisco would just as soon drill you as not, but I wanted it this way so you'd have a chance."

"Thanks for looking out for me, Hap," Reardon murmured.

He didn't believe that the other three outlaws were in the barn. After what had happened in Knapp's room that morning, Hall would not trust Talley alone in the house if they had been expecting Reardon. He guessed, then, that another man was with Talley, and the instant he appeared in the doorway, he'd get a bullet, but he could not tell whether Talley was in on the deal or not.

"I kind of like it outside," Reardon said finally. "I've been thinking about you all the way down here. Look's to me like you're in a hell of a fix."

Silence for a moment. Then Talley said, "That's crazy talk, Dan. You're the one who's in a hell of a fix. Frisco says you're the only man in Gold Cup he was worried about. He allowed there'd be a posse, and they'd spend a week running around like a flock of chickens with their heads cut off, but you'd figger we'd get horses here. Or if you didn't you'd go on to Knapp's Hole. That right, Dan?"

"Just about. I knew you'd go by Knapp's Hole to get the U.P. money."

"By sunup we'll be a hell of a long ways from here. Come in with your hands up, and I'll get a rope on you. You won't have nothing worse than a pair of skinned wrists."

"I doubt that, Hap. Likewise I doubt that you'll ever leave here alive."

"How do you figger?"

"First place Frisco ain't a gent to forget what happened this morning. Second place, you boys have got a pile of dinero, and a three-way split goes farther than four. So you'll get a slug in your belly." Someone swore inside. It was Boomer Shay's voice.

❧ CHAPTER 17 ❧

IT was a trap. Shay was waiting in the cabin to kill Dan Reardon, but Talley's position was still a question. Again Reardon acted on impulse, knowing that this moment favored him as much as any which lay ahead. He said, "Hear that, Hap? Boomer knows what Frisco was aiming to do."

Reardon lunged through the door, gun palmed. Talley was standing just inside. Reardon butted him in the belly, driving wind out of him in an audible gasp. Talley went back and down. Reardon spilled sideways just as Shay's gun sounded, a thunderous blast in the confines of the small room.

Reardon snapped a quick shot at Shay, heard it rip through the outlaw. He rolled and held his fire, and for one tight moment there was no sound in the cabin but the rasp of a man's hard breathing. Talley lay motionless in front of the door, the twilight reaching in and falling across him. It was completely dark in the back of the room. The breathing might be coming from either Gebhardt or Shay.

Indecision gripped Reardon. Talley was stirring, still fighting for breath. Hall and Denboe would be outside, probably in the barn, but whether they would hold to their hiding-place or break across the yard and rush the cabin was a question in Reardon's mind. Then, suddenly, Shay fell, his body crashing against a table and onto the floor as if all controls had been lost at once.

Shay had not gone down like a man faking his fall, but Reardon had to be sure. He bellied across the room, made a wide swing of his left hand, found Shay's shoulder, and yanked him into the corner. He struck a match, the tiny flame raveling up into the darkness and reaching out to Shay's face. The outlaw was dead.

Talley was on his feet now, still laboring for breath. Reardon said, "Don't make a move, Hap. You're the one man in this outfit I don't want to kill."

"What'd you hit me with?" Talley asked.

"My head."

Talley grunted. "No wonder."

"Slide your gun across the floor," Reardon ordered.

"What the hell! I told you I wouldn't throw no lead at you."

"Let's have your iron."

Reardon had Talley pinned in the doorway, and Talley could not help knowing it. He hesitated as if debating whether he should obey, then pulled his gun and slid it across the floor. Reardon caught it and slipped it into his waistband.

"Frisco claimed you was a tough customer," Talley said in an aggrieved tone. "Looks like he was right, and I've been trying to keep you alive."

"Are you as tough as you're letting on?"

"I'm tough enough," Talley said sullenly, "but you've played hell. Nothing I can do now. Frisco will blow your heart out."

"Maybe I'll do the blowing."

Talley swore. "You're talking big. There's nobody in these parts who can handle Frisco."

"We'll see," Reardon said irritably. "I figger he ain't as much man as you claim."

"I saw him run the U.P. job," Talley flung back. "I've heard about him for years. A man don't get a reputation like he's got just by gabbing."

"Reputations are tricky, Hap. Remember what happened this morning. When you lined up beside me, he backed down."

"He didn't want no gun trouble. Not with the bank job waiting to be pulled off."

"You're sizing it up plumb wrong. He's just a good gambler. He didn't like the kind of odds it made."

"All right," Talley growled. "I ain't here to auger. I wanted to save your hide. Now nobody can save it."

"Nobody but me. Either you're lying, Hap, or you're a blind, trusting fool. Shay was waiting to plug me. Then they'd have got you. Frisco's the kind who won't stand for any of his outfit augering with him. He told you that this morning."

"He wouldn't have done anything," Talley said in the tone of a man trying to convince himself.

Reardon understood something then he hadn't before. It was hero worship on Talley's part, and that worship was probably the reason Talley had thrown in with Hall in the first place. Talley must have been forced to a difficult decision this morning. He had his ideas of right and wrong, badly twisted, but he had them, and they were strong enough to bring him to Reardon's side against the man he idealized.

It was not enough, Reardon was thinking, to save Pat Quinn's bank. He had to save Hap Talley, and this was his one chance. If the kid went on from here, there would be no turning back.

"Look, Hap," Reardon said. "You've had your fun. You've listened to the boys' talk. They've told you stories about the rest of the Wild Bunch. You've heard the good things about Butch Cassidy and the rest, but I doubt like hell that you've heard the other side."

"There ain't no other side," Talley said sullenly. "I know what a railroad is. I know what banks are. My dad lost his ranch on a mortgage and shot himself. Don't preach to me. If there's a damned fool around here, it's you for trying to take Quinn's money back to him."

"Now that might be," Reardon agreed, "but I'm thinking mostly about you. This isn't your life, Hap."

"The hell it ain't," Talley snapped.

"How did you feel when you were robbing the U.P.?"

"Fine. Most excitement I ever had."

"Sure, felt big, didn't you? But how was it when you were on the run, heading for Knapp's Hole, knowing you were a fair target for any trigger-happy yahoo you met up with? You couldn't sleep. You couldn't stop. You couldn't trust nobody."

Talley took a long breath. "I felt like hell," he admitted.

"All of them do. Don't let their brags fool you. You live a lifetime worrying about when somebody's gonna recognize you. You know there's a reward out and every bounty chaser in the country is on the lookout. Chances are you didn't sleep or get a square meal till you got to the Hole. The reason you liked working for me this summer was because you didn't have to watch your back trail all the time for some lawman to come riding through the brush."

"Wasn't just that," Talley grumbled. "We was figgering on this bank job."

"So now you're into it again," Reardon flung at him. "The same running and dodging and looking back, and if you stick with Hall, you've got to trust a man who'll sooner or later plug you because he ain't sure he can trust you."

"You're wasting your wind," Talley said sullenly.

"I don't think so," Reardon said in a low tone. "I'm calling it right, and you know I am, or Shay wouldn't have given himself away when I was outside."

Silence then. Reardon sensed that Talley was thinking

it over. The outlaw stood in the doorway, staring into the night, the faint wash of the starshine upon him. Suddenly he wheeled. "Damn it, Dan! What are you trying to do to me?"

"I'm trying to save you from a rope or a bullet in your guts. You'll get one or the other if you keep going this way." Reardon followed the wall to stand beside Talley. "Hap, you're on the square. If you weren't you wouldn't have sided me this morning, or you wouldn't have tried to save my neck with Hall. Right now you're deciding what the trail's gonna be for you. Take a look ahead and see if you want to live the rest of your life like you did when you left Desert Wells."

Then, because he could not take that look, Talley fell back on the same outlaw philosophy Reardon had heard the first night in the Hole. He muttered, "I figger anything I can get from a railroad or a bank is honest money."

"You know better," Reardon said hotly. "It ain't just Quinn I'm thinking about. If the bank goes under, what happens to the men and women of Gold Cup who had their money in Quinn's bank?"

"Aw, he won't go broke."

"Quinn won't, but he's crook enough to let the little fellow take the beating." Reardon paused, thinking of Quinn, and Ash Lane, and knowing that as long as he lived he'd fight the same battle he was fighting now. He plunged on. "Hap, I decided years ago that dying wasn't the worst thing a man could do. Living so you're afraid to look yourself in the face is a hell of a lot worse. Collie found that out."

"Yeah," Talley grunted. "I wouldn't want to live like

Collie did."

"Keep going and that's where you'll wind up."

"I can't do nothing else, Dan. When a man gets out of line once, he's finished."

"Not unless he wants to be. Who knows you were in this deal?"

"Nobody but you and the boys. I was below town cutting the wires when Frisco and Boomer pulled the job off. Monte was outside with the horses."

"All right then. Now I aim to get the bank's money back to Quinn. Your job's to return the U.P. dinero. From then on you can live the way you want to."

"Nobody knew I was in that U.P. job neither," Talley muttered. "We had our faces masked. Reckon I'll keep my part of it."

"Turn it back to the railroad," Reardon said sharply. "You'll never feel right if you don't. You'll be Collie all over again."

"Mebbe," Talley breathed. "Mebbe."

Talley was silent then, and Reardon, knowing he had said enough, let the outlaw have his thoughts. From here on out, Hap Talley must make his own decision. Reardon sensed the conflict that was going on in his mind. He had proof that Talley liked and respected him, but he knew, too, how great was his worship for Frisco Hall's ruthless and lawless daring. It was impossible to reconcile a loyalty to two men as different as Hall and Reardon. Talley must, then, be brought to his decision by some inner sense of values.

Suddenly Talley dropped a hand to Reardon's arm, squeezed a warning, and pulled it away. Reardon had heard nothing. It was black-dark now; the wild smell of this country was in the air. There was the steady dribble of water into the horse trough over by the barn, the hoot of an owl, the whisper of the San Miguel beyond the haystacks. That was all, yet Reardon knew Talley had caught something he had missed. With that warning gesture, Hap Talley had made his decision.

Then Reardon saw it, a faint moving shadow to his right; he heard a scuffing sound of someone pulling himself through the dust. Reardon fired at the shadow, the shot breaking into the night silence and setting up a series of echoes that beat against the sides of the canyon. He stepped out of the doorway and stood with his back to the wall. A man cried out in agony and fired. Reardon ran at him, shooting, and the shadowy bulk of the outlaw dropped flat.

Another man was running back to the corrals, calling, "Frisco." Reardon raced toward the barn. There was little loyalty in these men when their luck ran out. If Denboe could get clear with the money, he'd take off, and Reardon would have to start the chase again. He reached the barn, heard a door squeak open, and laid a shot along it. Denboe answered the shot and slid inside.

Reardon had been in Gebhardt's barn. He pictured it now, the wall with its harness hanging from pegs on one side, the long runway, the series of stalls. There was only the one door. Reardon reloaded his gun and, moving along the wall to the door, stood listening. He heard nothing.

"Come on out, Monte," Reardon called. "It's the money I want. Not you."

No answer. A wind began moving down the canyon.

Reardon heard it in the trees along the river. A boulder broke loose high up on the south wall and roared down the precipitous slope, crashing through the brush and small trees until it hit the river. The echoes died, and there was silence again except for the wind.

Reardon's nerves squeezed him. He was a man who had never found waiting easy. Now it was intolerable. Only Monte Denboe was left, for there had been no movement from Frisco Hall since Reardon had shot him. Because he could wait no longer, Reardon dropped flat and crawled past the door. He lay in the opening; very still, the night pressing around him.

It was, Reardon knew, a test of patience, and not the kind of thing he did well. If he rose, whatever light there was would be against him. If he crawled into the barn, some small sound would betray his position. Still, it was not in him to wait. His middle had gone empty; sweat burst through his skin as he felt the keen stab of regret. He liked Monte Denboe. Now he must kill him, or be killed.

Carefully Reardon reached for the door, gripped it, and pulled it toward him. Rusty hinges squeaked dismally into the silence, a terrible sound sawing on tight nerves. It broke Denboe. He fired, gun thunder racketing into the night. Spurts of flame marked his position at the far end of the runway.

Bullets snapped over Reardon, hip-high on a standing man. Reardon took one shot, dived inside and away from the door, and fired twice. Denboe had let go four times. Now his gun was silent, and when the hammering echoes were gone, Reardon heard his rasping breathing, but only for a moment.

Reardon moved along the runway, dried sweat stinging his face, barn and powder smells thick and repellent. He stumbled over Denboe's body, struck a match, and looked at him. He turned away, sick, thinking of Denboe's good laugh. Another year or two and Hap Talley would be lying somewhere like this unless he held to the decision he had made when he had warned Reardon.

Another match showed the money tied to one of the saddles. Reardon cut it loose just as Talley came into the barn, calling, "Where are you, Dan?"

Strange, Reardon thought, that Talley would be so sure he was the one still on his feet. He said, "Here, Hap," and moved to the door. "Come back to Gold Cup with me."

"The hell I will," Talley cried in a ragged voice. "I'm heading out of here."

Talley plunged around the corner of the barn and returned with his horse. He found a lantern, lighted it, and lifting his saddle off one of Gebhardt's horses, dropped it on his own. In the murky light his face seemed old, mouth drawn tight against his teeth, skin as gray as a goose wing.

He did not look at Reardon until he was in the saddle. When he did put his eyes on Reardon, there was puzzlement in them, and resentment. Within the hour, Reardon thought, Talley's way of life had been destroyed. Three men whom he had considered superior in fighting skill and cold courage to anyone else had gone down before one man's gun.

But no bitterness was apparent in Talley, no hatred. Now, in this brief moment when their eyes met, Reardon wondered if he regretted the warning gesture he had made in the doorway of Gebhardt's cabin. He wondered, too, if

Talley understood that he had, perhaps without conscious thought, chosen his side when he had made the gesture.

"I want my gun," Talley said.

Reardon handed it to him without a word.

Talley said, "So long, Dan," and rode out of the barn.

"So long," Reardon called. "I'll be back in Long Tom Valley in a few days."

Talley did not say anything. A moment later he was in the road and the brittle, clacking sound of his passage came back to Reardon.

Gebhardt, Reardon found, was conscious and straining at his ropes. Reardon freed him, saw that he had nothing worse than a headache, and told him what had happened. Then he said, "I've got to get this dinero back to Gold Cup. There's three dead men around here. You'd better tote 'em into Placerville."

Leaving the cabin, Reardon crossed the clearing to his horse. Pulling himself into the saddle, he paused long enough to roll and light a cigarette, but he found no pleasure in it. Tired and oppressed by what had happened, he felt small and futile, his senses dull, and the question of what it was worth began to plague him. Then he put his horse through the brush to the road, and turned upstream to follow the singing river.

❦ CHAPTER 18 ❦

IT was not yet dawn when Reardon rode into Gold Cup. The mining camp lay silent before him, Main Street deserted, with only here and there a lamp throwing a long yellow finger of light across the gray, thick dust.

There were no barkers crying the pleasures to be found in the Gold Palace or the other saloons and gambling-halls that crowded the street, no rumble from Pat Quinn's great stamp mill up the river, not even a drunk's thick-tongued song to break the silence.

Overhead stars glittered in the slit of sky wedged in between the towering peaks that lifted granite heads above the spruce. Even the wind, never entirely absent, was only a caress as it breathed down the canyon. Now, for a few hours out of the twenty-four, Gold Cup slept.

Reardon reined into the livery stable, woke the hostler, and walked back into the street, the sack of money gripped in his left hand. He was bone weary, his numbed brain refusing to react coherently. He should get Quinn out of bed and hand the money to him. Then it would be the banker's responsibility. But he didn't. Stumbling, his legs stiff, he crossed the hotel lobby, climbed the stairs, and went into his room.

It seemed a month since he had slept. Locking the door, he shoved a chair under the knob and laid the sack of money on the bed. He pulled off his boots, shrugged out of his coat, and lifting his gun from leather, dropped it beside the sack. Then, still fully dressed except for his boots, he fell across the bed, one arm flung out over the money, and sleep dragged him down into a black sea.

There was a banging on his door and a loud voice, "All right, Reardon. Open up, or we're coming in."

Reardon thought, in that first moment, that he was dreaming. He heard the pulsing beat of the stamp mill, became aware of the sharp sunlight on his face. Then there was a crashing racket, the door was smashed open, and men boiled into the room, a million of them, it seemed. This was no dream.

Grabbing his gun, Reardon sat up. Dry lips moved. "Stand pat, or I'll blow some heads off."

His eyes refused to focus. The marshal was in front. Damn it, there were three of them, all with stars on their shirts, lined up beside each other, the three exactly alike. He hadn't known before that the lawman he'd pulled out of the saddle the day before had two brothers. They must be triplets.

They stopped, the marshals spread across the room at the foot of his bed. All spoke at once. "We got the news in early this morning, Reardon. Gebhardt brought the men in you'd killed and wired from Placerville. One of 'em, got away. He said there was four in the outfit."

"What the hell you busting in here for?" Reardon demanded.

Now there was only one marshal staring at Reardon, grim distaste curling his lips. "What'd you do with the money?"

"I've got it here and I'm taking it to Quinn. Your horse is in the Red Front stable. Now get out before I start making some smoke."

The men behind the marshal moved to the door, but the lawman held his place, scratching his neck, disappointment in him. "It may be I had you wrong, mister. I figgered you'd cache that dinero and come back with a cock-and-bull yarn about failing to find it. Or mebbe claiming the fellow who got away took it."

"You had me wrong all right," Reardon said darkly. "Pat ain't lost anything. Now you sloping out of here?"

"Yeah. I'll wait in the hall and go with you to the bank just to be sure you get there."

The marshal turned on his heel and tramped out. Reardon swung his feet to the floor, and rubbed his face. He felt like the last piece of wash that had just gone through the wringer. Rising, he walked across the room, poured water into a basin, and made the mistake of looking into the cracked mirror. He grimaced, shut his eyes, and looked again.

"I don't know you," he said to the face in the mirror, "and I don't want to. You're ugly enough to scare the stink out of a skunk."

He sloshed water over his face, rubbed his eyes, and dried. Turning back to the bed, he pulled on his boots, buckled his gun belt around him, and slapped his hat on his head. He slid into his coat and, with the sack of money in his left hand, walked into the hall.

The marshal said, "You took your time."

"That's one thing I've got plenty of." Reardon's eyes locked with the lawman's. "Friend, I don't like you. Chances are you've let Link Bellew get out of town, still claiming that murder ain't murder."

"I ain't looking for Bellew," the marshal flung back, "and I ain't bowed down under my load of affection for you. Now get along."

"Start out."

"I'll walk behind you."

Reardon's laugh was a dry, grating sound. "Friend, when I let a gent like you walk behind me, I'm going to be a hell of a lot worse off than I am now."

Anger hit the lawman. He started to reach for his gun

and instantly changed his mind. He had remembered, Reardon guessed wryly, the three bodies Gebhardt had brought to Placerville. Without a word, the marshal wheeled and stomped down the stairs, Reardon following.

They left the hotel, the crowd pressing around them. Questions were flung at Reardon. He ignored them, reached the bank, and went in. Quinn was at his desk, a bandage around his head. He looked up, saw who it was, and rose.

"So help me, Dan," Quinn said. "I didn't think you'd pull it off."

"You always peg me a little low." Reardon dropped the sack on the desk. "I didn't count this dinero, but I think it's all here."

The banker spilled the money on his desk, pleased. "Well, I'm thanking you, son. The sheriff was off on another case, and Lacey here allowed he had to stay in town. They had the damnedest time getting a posse together." He laughed. "I'll bet they're still riding and looking." He spread the currency out. "I'll count this after while, but looks like it's here all right. Big bills, mostly. They didn't take time to clean me out, but they got away with about thirty thousand."

"Three of 'em were beefed," the marshal said. "That left one to ride out. I'm wondering how that happened. Mebbe you'd better make the count now."

Wheeling, Reardon hit the lawman on the side of the head, the sound of the blow running the length of the room. The marshal crashed into the wall, and his feet slid out from under him.

"I'm done taking that kind of gab," Reardon said flatly.

"Yesterday you couldn't go after 'em, but you were all for throwing me into the jug. Now keep your damned mouth shut."

Hate tightened Lacey's face; it burned in his eyes, but he didn't make a move toward his gun. He said, "I'd like nothing better'n to jug this hombre, Pat. Now count that dinero."

Men packed in the doorway stared expectantly. Quinn waved them out of the bank. "Git. You ain't gonna see nothing." When they had gone, he said, "You're making a fool out of yourself, Lacey." Raising his voice he called, "Meyers."

A man came into the office and began to count with Quinn. Reardon moved around the desk and stood with his shoulder blades pressed against the wall, head lowered, eyes on Lacey. The marshal was on his feet, one hand feeling of his face, ignoring Reardon's stare.

Later Quinn said, "All here, Lacey. Let Reardon alone. You're sore because he took your horse. If he hadn't, the bank wouldn't have this money. Now git."

The marshal wheeled out of the room, the crack of his spike heels pistol-sharp on the floor. Quinn grinned. "Don't work up no ruckus with him, Dan. He's a good man mostly. Just don't like for the other fellow to get any glory." He flipped the lid of the cigar box back and shoved it toward Reardon. "Who was it got away?"

Reardon shook his head at the cigar box and lifted tobacco and paper from his shirt pocket. "Talley, the one I called Jones."

"He's the young one?"

Reardon nodded. "That's the one. Pat, you owe me

something."

Quinn had reached for a cigar. He held it in front of him, irritation washing through him. "That's a funny thing for you to say. You know damned well I'll give you anything I've got. I told you I'd stake you and Astha to a honeymoon—"

"I don't mean that. I figger you owe me two things. Take Talley. He didn't have nothing to do with the holdup. He wasn't even in town at the time. He did me a good turn yesterday when Hall was fixing to jump me, and I'd like to return the favor."

Quinn bit off the end of his cigar, good humor returning to him. "You're saying you don't want me to get a warrant out for him." He picked up a handful of bills. "I haven't lost anything, Dan. Hell, I don't want Talley. Maybe he'll see he's on the wrong track."

"I figger he will. The other thing is Ash Lane. I want you to give him more time."

Quinn had struck a match to light his cigar. Now he stared at Reardon as if unable to believe what he'd heard. The flame ran up the stick and burned his fingers. Swearing, he waved it out. He said, "My ears must be playing me tricks. Say that over."

"Give Lane more time. You heard it straight."

Quinn rose, big hands clutching the ends of the desk, his face suddenly purple. "You damned fool. You know that's the one thing I won't do. Anything you want but that."

"That's what it's got to be. I told you in the beginning that smashing Ash wasn't in the game. I aimed to whittle him down, but wiping him out on account of a two-bit debt ain't right."

"It ain't right," Quinn jeered. "Now who in hell cares whether it's right or not? What do you think I went to all this trouble for? I'll make something on the beef you fetched, but that ain't the point. I operate for more than one year's profit. I look ahead. Always have. I want Long Tom Valley. All of it, and I'll start with Broken Bell. Then I'll run the little fry out. You'll be the big cheese just like Lane's been, but we'll have a spread that'll make Broken Bell look like a ten-cow outfit."

Reardon shook his head. "I won't stand for it, Pat."

In a sudden gust of rage, Quinn threw his cigar across the room. "In case you've forgotten, Reardon, let me remind you who you are. I picked you up and let you in on this deal because Astha liked you and because I took to the way you were bucking Lane. You had twenty steers and a little cow-and-calf herd, and Lane was fixing to wipe you out. Now you've got money in your pocket and you're marrying into the biggest fortune on the western slope. All I'm asking is to let me run this show. You don't owe Lane a damned thing. Forget him."

"I don't owe him nothing for a fact," Reardon conceded, "but I'll keep the right to run my own show, and this started out like it was mine. Whittling Ash down by taking his market away from him is one thing, but stealing everything he's got is something else."

Quinn dropped into his chair, hands fisted in front of him, pulse throbbing in his temples. "Dan, let's get one thing straight now. You're my partner. You'll be my son-in-law, but, by hell, there's one thing I won't stand from nobody. That's getting kicked back to second fiddle in my own orchestra."

"Looks to me like it's time somebody did some kicking around here," Reardon said.

Quinn motioned toward the door. "Git. Go on before I tell Astha she picked the wrong man."

"I'll be back," Reardon said, and wheeled out of the office.

❧ CHAPTER 19 ❧

REARDON crossed the street to a restaurant and had breakfast. It was the first meal he'd eaten for twenty-four hours, but he was not hungry. He ate automatically, thinking briefly of Collie Knapp and his words: "Your way of meeting problems head on is the only way." Now Reardon wondered. He was putting his head down and ramming into this one. He knew that, foolish or not, he'd bull it through to whatever end the future held.

He paid for his meal and went directly to the Conner House. Ash Lane was in the lobby talking to Sue when Reardon came in. Hearing the door, he turned. Reardon said, "Howdy, Ash."

For an instant the old cowman stood motionless, shirt front stirred by his breathing. He was a different man than the arrogant Ash Lane Reardon had known. His hands trembled at his sides, his long-beaked face was lined by suffering, and he stood awkwardly with his weight on one leg.

Lane's pride had been beaten down by the knowledge that he had found no escape from the destiny Pat Quinn had shaped for him. He stood within days of destruction, but one thing in him had not changed. He had spent these months hating Dan Reardon. Now that hate jolted the one word, "Reardon," out of him as if it were an oath, and made him reach for his gun.

Sue grabbed his arm, crying, "No, Dad, no."

Lane flung her back against the wall, shouting, "I'll kill you, Reardon."

"Not today, Ash." Reardon's gun was in his hand and lined on Lane's chest. "My father used to say that success made some men's heads swell like a bloated cow's belly. That's the way you are. You've got so big in the head you're loco."

Lane glared at Reardon. He breathed, "Maybe not today, but I'll have my chance. When I do, I'll blow your heart out. If it wasn't for you, I wouldn' be in this shape."

"Don't blame me for your bull head," Reardon said sharply. "You ain't even smart. You've got where you are by riding other people down, and now you're getting some of your own medicine. You and Pat Quinn are like two peas in the same pod, the only difference being that you're the little one."

"Do you have to talk to him like that?" Sue cried.

"That's not all I've got to say, but the rest'll wait. Ash, how much do you owe Quinn?"

"None of your damned business," Lane raged. "Go ask your partner. Ask the father of the floozie you're fixing to marry."

Reardon struck him on the side of the head with an open palm, the sound of the blow ringing sharply across the lobby. "You'll keep a decent tongue in your head when I'm doing you a favor."

Lane backed against the wall, hand lifted to his cheek. Still, with his luck run out, Ash Lane did not break. "I want no favors from you. You've been taking big steps this summer, Reardon. Too damned big, but I'll get my chance. You'll see."

"You'll get your chance when every ten-cow rancher and settler in Long Tom Valley gets off his knees. I won't ask you again. How much do you owe Quinn?"

"Seven thousand," Sue answered. "That's interest and principal on two notes that are due in a few days, and the interest on the mortgage Quinn holds on Broken Bell."

"All right," Reardon said. "Ash, we're paying Quinn a visit. Keep your hands off your gun. It'd look like hell to push you down the street with a cutter in your back."

For a long moment Lane stared at Reardon, great bald head thrust forward, a long-beaked eagle with his tail feathers pulled. Reardon holstered his gun. Without another word Lane limped past Reardon into the street.

They went down the plank walk, Lane stumbling like a man drunk on his anger, Sue with her head high, and Reardon watching for Link Bellew. He had seen nothing of the Broken Bell foreman since Collie Knapp's death, but he was not sure the man had left Gold Cup.

Suddenly Lane turned to face Reardon. "If Link was in town, this'd be a different show."

"You saying Link ain't around?"

"He left early this morning," Sue said.

"Well now," Reardon murmured, "that was right lucky for Link. Sue tell you why he was here, Ash?"

"I don't believe it," Lane said bitterly. "Just another of

Knapp's—" Something in Reardon's eyes made him stop. He cleared his throat. "Link came to Gold Cup to see if I'd found a market for our beef."

"Did you?"

"You know the answer to that as well as I do. Good thing he came. I told him to hold the herd at Placerville. We'll ship to Denver."

"Did he tell you why he left town?"

"He went back to stop the herd, I told you."

"Now mebbe he went back so he'd live a few days more. When you see him, tell him to start smoking his iron if he ever meets up with me again."

"I'll be glad to tell him," Lane said. "I'll be right glad."

Reardon nodded at the bank. "Get moving, Ash. When we're inside, you do what I tell you without letting Quinn know I'm making you do it."

Lane went on, holding his silence. Sue looked questioningly at Reardon, but he told her nothing. They walked through the bank and on to Quinn's office; Reardon, stepping aside for Sue to go in ahead of him, then followed.

Quinn looked up from his desk, scowling. "Paying up, are you, Lane?"

"That's right," Reardon said. "Get out Ash's notes, Pat. He's taking 'em up. Likewise he's paying the interest on the mortgage you hold."

Without a word Quinn rose, walked to the safe, and returned with a long envelope. "I'm not surprised, Dan," he said, "judging from what you said a while ago, but it's damned hard to believe you'd change sides like this."

"I'm not changing sides," Reardon said quietly, "and

I'll keep the bargain I made."

Quinn sat down at his desk, eyes searching Reardon's face. "Now what bargain would you have in mind?"

"With Astha." Reardon stripped off his money belt and, removing the bills Quinn had given him the morning before, laid them on the desk in front of Lane. "Count out what you need, Ash."

Quinn's face held none of his usual good humor. He said contemptuously, "Funny what can make a tolerably bright man do a fool thing like you're doing now. Maybe it's her." He, jabbed a thumb at Sue. "If you're working around to get out of marrying Astha, you've sure done the job. I can forgive a man for almost anything except being the kind of idiot who scrapes the butter off the bread I've spread for him." He picked up the bills Lane had thrown across the desk. "Paying me off with my own money. Now ain't that a good one?"

Quinn scratched *Paid* across the notes, wrote a receipt for the interest, and handed it and the canceled notes to Lane. "All right, Ash. Maybe you'd like to play a little more poker before you leave camp."

"No." Lane pocketed the notes and receipt and handed the rest of Reardon's money back to him. "I had enough last year."

Quinn grinned. "I didn't think you'd want any more, but it don't make much difference. You'll never sell another steer in Gold Cup. What's more, I doubt that you'll even own any when you get back to the valley."

Lane stared at the banker, puzzled and bewildered. "What are you driving at?"

The grin still lingered in the corners of Quinn's mouth.

"I'm a careful man, Ash. I wouldn't be where I am today if I didn't figure all the ways the other fellow could play his hand. I knew there was a chance you could scrape up seven thousand, although I didn't expect it to come from Reardon. Besides, a few of the butchers hereabout don't like my way of doing things. So I made arrangements for your beef to go the other way."

"What the hell are you talking about?" Lane shouted. "My herd's on the trail now. I told Bellew to hold my beef at Placerville. I'm shipping to Denver."

Quinn's laugh was a slapping taunt. "You made a mistake when you didn't take my offer last spring. Around here they talk about Pat Quinn's luck. I make my luck, Ash. My method is to provide for any leak my original plan might spring later on." He picked up a cigar from his desk and bit off the end, good humor flowing back into his muscle-ridged face. "You're just like one of your bulls, Ash. You get your eyes on a piece of grass and you can't see nothing else."

Sue came to stand beside her father, face pale. "You've had your fun, Quinn. What are you trying to say?"

"I'll tell you, ma'am. Your dad trusted Bellew. No matter what happens, he keeps right on trusting him because he's so damned sure he knows it all. That's a mistake. I never trust a man until he's in as deep as I am. I didn't even trust Reardon like Ash has been trusting Bellew. He paid Bellew a ramrod's wages, but that's not good enough for Link. No sir!" He leaned forward, cigar tilted upward. "When you get back to the valley, you won't have no more trail herd than a jack rabbit. Bellew will have it over the La Sals."

"You're lying." Fear squeezed Lane's features. "Link may have taken your money, which same makes you the sucker, but he wouldn't sell me out."

"You don't think so?" Quinn shrugged thick shoulders. "Now you go ahead and believe what you want to. You can even believe that Bellew came up here to find out if you'd lined up some buyers like he said, but if you're smart, you'll believe me when I say he came to make a deal with me. I paid him to get that herd out of the valley. That'll make a right profitable deal for your friend, Ash. Besides what I paid him, he'll have the herd to sell."

Lane turned and stumbled out of the room. Sue said with withering contempt, "The outlaws who held up your bank are honest men compared to you." Whirling, she ran after her father.

"Honest outlaws." Quinn winked at Reardon. "Funny thing, Dan. You and me are more alike than I thought. I'm sorry it's gone this way because we'd have made a good team. You took this deal, made love to Astha, put on a fine face, and all the time you aimed to pull enough out of it to save Lane's hide so you'd get a chunk of Broken Bell."

"You've got that a little wrong," Reardon said sharply.

"No use to lie now," Quinn went on. "It's water under the bridge. I had some doubts about you last spring when we left the valley. You see, Astha's after a certain kind of man. You came pretty near filling the bill, but she made one bad mistake. She wanted a fighter, and you're that, but she likewise wanted a man she could dress up and make live in a fine house in Denver. Parade him around in front of the big bugs and be proud of him. It won't work. Now you stay away from Astha. You'll never be anything but a cowhand if you live to be a million."

"That's right," Reardon agreed, and wheeled out of the office.

He caught up with the Lanes before they reached the Conner House. He said, "I'll get back to the valley as soon as I can, Ash. Bellew had several irons in the fire on this trip. I figger he might be double-crossing Quinn."

Lane kept on toward the Conner House, refusing to look at Reardon. Sue said, "You've done a lot for us, Dan. We can't go on expecting favors from you. It's up to Dad now."

"Nothing's up to me," Lane said evenly. "I told Link to have the herd at Placerville. It'll be there."

"Well I'll be damned." Reardon grabbed Lane's shoulder and swung him around. "You mean you still can't see through Bellew?"

Lane jerked free. "I see through you, Reardon. You ain't so smart, paying Quinn off. I owe you seven thousand. All right. You'll get it back, but nothing's changed as far as you're concerned. Don't you forget that. Knapp's dead, and that's the way it should be. There won't be no more stolen horses coming through the valley. I said I'd run you out of the country, and I will as sure as hell's hot."

"I was wrong last spring," Sue said bitterly. "I told Dan that you two were like a couple of bulls butting your heads against each other. I was wrong, Dad. It's like Quinn said. You're the one that acts like a bull."

"I got where I am by hard work," Lane cried in an outraged tone. "I don't aim to have Dan Reardon for a partner just because he was sharp enough to make seven thousand dollars this summer. That's what he's been working for all the time, and don't tell me different." He swallowed, fighting down the anger that was like a fire in his veins. "I never made a mistake in a man. I didn't make one in Bellew."

"You'll never change, will you, Ash?" Reardon said. "I guess I don't want to be your partner no more than you want me, but there's one thing I've wanted from the first. I saved your hide with Quinn, and that ought to give me an interest in Broken Bell."

"The hell it does," Lane shouted. "You're getting out of the valley. Send me your address and I'll mail the seven thousand to you."

"Until you pay me," Reardon said doggedly, "I've got that interest. I told you there was one thing I wanted, and I'll have it. You'll quit playing God for the valley and let every man that lives there get up off his knees."

Lane's face was gray. His breathing seemed a great effort. He said, "Reardon, you've used a gun on me today. You've ridden me and you've raked me with your spurs. Ain't that enough?"

"Not quite," Reardon said.

He left them there on the plank walk and turned into a barbershop. He still hadn't seen Astha.

❧ CHAPTER 20 ❧

ASTHA gave her hair a final pat and changed from a maroon robe to a blue silk dress. It was nearly noon, and her father would be home shortly to eat with her. He might know when Dan was coming, for she had heard Dan was back in Gold Cup with the money that had been stolen from the bank, and her impatience to see him had grown by the minute. If he did not come soon, she would go to him. Pride was not important now. She had to know how he felt about her.

She gave a look around the room. The rosewood furniture was the best that could be bought in Denver. The big bathroom finished in Italian marble was probably the finest on the western slope. She smiled. Dan would not like this kind of thing at first, but he would when he became used to it. Her father had, and his life had been as rough as Dan Reardon's. Frowning, she crossed to a window, wondering about Dan. It had been almost two days since he had delivered the herd, and he had not been to see her. Then she remembered he had been gone most of that time after the outlaws who had robbed the bank. That, she told herself quickly, was the reason he had not been to see her.

Opening a window, she felt the chill bite of the air. The rumble of the stamp mill came to her, stirring the silence as it did every waking hour. She hated it. From here she could look down upon the town with its crowded Main Street. As soon as it was dark the cry of the barkers could be heard up here on the hill, the oaths and yells of the miners, the bawdy songs.

She hated all of it; she hated everything about Gold Cup. This was where the money that she loved to spend came from, but there was no reason for her to live here. Even the quiet of Long Tom Valley and Dan's tiny cabin would be a relief. But she would not live there long. She had always been able to make her father do what she wanted. A husband should be no more difficult.

Looking down into the yard, she felt another wave of distaste. There had been a time when she loved it, the great iron fence and the trees that gave all the privacy of a king's palace grounds, the lawn and the few flowers that bloomed briefly in the short summer. She had liked the white-marble fish pool, the sundial with the letter Q carved on all four sides. She didn't like either of them now. Nor did she like the fountains. The angel on a mushroom. The lion spewing water through his mouth. The wild fowl with wings spread.

Astha had loved everything about the house and the yard because it was proof of Quinn power and wealth. That was the reason her father had built it. She had been young then, young enough to think she was in love with Mark Sands. But the years had taught her one thing. She could never be happy here. To live in Gold Cup was to be buried. What was the good of being wealthy if there were only miners and freighters and prospectors to stare at this evidence of Quinn money? They knew about the Quinns; they did not need proof.

It had been a mistake to build a house like this in Gold Cup. It was wasted, as out of place as a diamond ring on a mucker's finger. Some day there would be a house in Denver that would make the Quinn name as well known as Tabor.

She heard the clatter of Pat Quinn's buggy coming up the hill. She watched him make the wide swing below the house and come on through the great arched gateway. Smiling, she left her room and went down the curved stairway, not sure why she felt about her father as she did. Perhaps it was because she had no memory of her mother and Pat Quinn had made her the center of his life, but whatever the reason, she loved him as she loved no one else in the world. Her smile deepened. No one except Dan Reardon.

She waited in the dining-room. Her father was gone to the bank before she got up in the morning, and more often than not he stayed down town for supper, so they made it a rule to eat the noon meal together. Hearing him come in, she moved quickly across the room to stand beside the French doors. He liked to see her there with the sunlight upon her black hair. Usually he stopped and told her she was beautiful. But he did not today. He slammed the door and stood spread-legged, glaring at her as if she had been guilty of something too terrible to mention aloud.

"You sure as hell picked the wrong man," Quinn said finally in a flaying tone he had never used on her before.

She flinched, not understanding. Then anger touched her. "Don't use that bullwhip of a tongue on me. I don't work for you. Maybe that's what's wrong with Dan."

He wiped a hand across his face. "Sorry, Astha." He came around the table to her. "But we've figgered on this for almost a year and we thought we had everything accounted for. We just didn't read Reardon right. Or you didn't."

"What did he do?"

"Wanted me to give Lane more time. When I said no, he brought Lane and the girl in and picked up the old man's notes. Used my money to save Lane's hide. Not that it makes a hell of a lot of difference. Bellew will steal the herd, and in the end we'll have Broken Bell, but I don't like to wait."

She stared at him, not comprehending for a moment what he said. Then she laughed a little shakily. "Well, it proves just what I told you. You can't treat Dan like you would a man who works for you."

"I didn't. He's just stubborn, and he ain't smart enough to see which is the big end of the stick." He rubbed his chin, suddenly thoughtful. "He told me he said something to you about not going along with me. Why didn't you tell me?"

She hesitated, wondering whether she should lie, and deciding against it. "I thought it would be better not to. All I want is to get married, Dad. He'll come around. Give me time."

Quinn shook his head. "You can marry any of a dozen men here in town who'll follow orders. Reardon's not for you."

"You're wrong, Dad," she said simply. "I love him."

"Love him," he jeered. "Look, honey. We ain't been bothered much by love. We've worked fine together because we've known what we wanted, and now I'm damned if I'll let Reardon throw a monkey wrench into things. I told him to let you alone. You're finished with him."

She put a hand to her throat. "You told him to let me alone?"

"That's what I said. I've been thinking that maybe getting married would be the wrong thing. There's been many a time when you helped me swing a man the way I wanted him. I guess that's the way we'd better keep it."

"No," she screamed in a sudden rush of rage. "I'm done with that. I want one man, not a dozen that you need to do your dirty work. Dan's right. We've got enough without taking Lane's ranch away from him."

He dropped into a chair, hand automatically moving toward the cigars in his coat pocket. "What's got into you?"

"I'm just tired of all this scheming and plotting. I'm tired of throwing myself at men I don't like. I'm tired of robbing people so we'll be richer."

"Robbing people, eh?" His laugh was not a pleasant sound. "Looks like you've grown a conscience at the age of thirty. Ain't that a little late?"

"You can forget I'm thirty." Her mouth was an ugly red line across her face. "I married Mark because you needed a man to run your bunch of toughs. Somebody to do the dirty murdering jobs you couldn't do because it would have looked bad for the great Patrick Quinn to get mixed up in things like that. All right. It's past and it didn't work. This time I'll see that it's different."

"It'll be different all right," he shouted. "You'll live in a one-room shack in Long Tom Valley. You'll have twenty kids and break your fingernails on a washboard. I won't even buy you a Christmas present. You'll see how much of a fine house you have in Denver."

It was the nearest they had ever come to a serious quarrel. They glared at each other, their wills clashing. Neither heard the clatter of the brass knocker on the front door; neither knew that anyone had come in until the housekeeper opened the sitting-room door.

"There's a man out here, Miss Astha. Says his name is Reardon."

Quinn cursed and got up. "I'll throw him—"

"No you won't. I'll try to fix what you've broken." Whirling, she left the room.

The housekeeper had taken Reardon into the library. When Astha came in, he swung to her. She stopped, pleasure at seeing him rushing through her like the warmth of a strong drink.

"Oh, Dan, I thought you'd never come."

She ran across the room to him, forgetting all the things she had learned about handling men. She put her arms around him, not waiting for his advance, and kissed him long and passionately. When she drew away, she threw her head back and looked at him, smiling. She had stirred him as she always had when she kissed him, and she was pleased.

"Let's sit down." She tucked his hand through the crook of her arm and led him to the orange love seat in the corner. "How are you, Dan?"

"A mite sleepy," he said.

"The job's done. Why don't you sleep the clock around?"

"No, the job ain't done," he said moodily. "Maybe it never will be. Mebbe you go on fighting till somebody plugs you. I guess nothing is ever settled." He told her about the way Collie Knapp had died. "I saw him a little while ago. He never looked as peaceful when he was alive."

He wiped a hand across his forehead as if he found it hard to think. He was thinner than he had been in July. His clothes were new; he was freshly shaved, and his hair had just been cut, but it took a moment for her to see that there were greater differences in him than these superficial ones that were immediately apparent. His nerves were pulled tight; constant tension had honed his temper to a fine edge, and he seemed harder than she remembered him, more aloof, taciturn, almost bitter. His mood came, she thought, from Knapp's death.

She sat close to him, a leg pressed against his, her full red lips holding the wistful smile that she had learned long ago was a potent weapon to use on a man when his emotions were tangled.

"It's been a century since I saw you," she said softly. "I've planned a hundred things for us when I was living through that century. You don't have to go on fighting, you know, and you don't have to die to find peace. I'll bring it to you."

A crooked grin touched his mouth. "That ain't the way I got it from Pat a while ago. He said to let you alone."

"Oh, he's mad because Lane got away from him. You were the one who sprung the trap, so he's mad at you. Let me handle him. I always bring him around."

Reardon rose and moved across the room to the desk. "Where did this come from?"

He was getting at something, but she couldn't tell what it was. She realized, in that moment, that he possessed a quality she did not understand, a depth of character, perhaps, a desire for something far less casual than the physical appetites of the men she had known intimately. She had become an expert at satisfying these appetites, but now she was puzzled. She said carefully, "It came from France. It belonged to Louis the Sixteenth."

He ran a hand across the smooth surface. "I suppose it cost a thousand dollars."

Wondering what was in his mind, she lied. "Yes, it cost about that."

"Have you read those?" He waved at the shelves of books.

"No, I haven't." She laughed softly as if the books were a joke. "Neither has Dad, but they make a good show."

"You've got an education," he said. "You've read some of them."

"Oh, a few. Dad sent me to school in Denver, but I know one thing. You're better educated than I am."

He gave her that small crooked grin again and moved on to the punch bowl made from gold taken from the American Girl mine. "It's worth a fortune." He motioned toward the costly collection of Venetian glassware. "I don't know about those gadgets, but they look like more money." He swung to face her. "You're used to all this, Astha, but I'm not. There couldn't be any peace for either one of us if we got married."

"That's the craziest thing I ever heard you say," she cried indignantly. "I've told you before. I'd be happy just married to you."

He shook his head. "Pat told me something today. He said you thought you could get me to Denver and dress me up in a silk shirt and a good suit, and show me off. It was a crazy idea in the first place because I'm nothing to show off, but even if it wasn't crazy, I wouldn't stand for it, and you'd never let me pull you down to what I've got."

"It wouldn't be pulling me down. Last spring—"

"Yeah, I watched you cook a couple of meals and I

fooled myself. Maybe I wanted to fool myself because Sue and me had had a ruckus, but I'm not now. Pat said this morning I'd never be anything but a cowhand. That's it."

She rose and crossed the room to him. He was right when he said that he'd wanted to fool himself because he'd broken up with Sue. She had realized that from the first. Then it had seemed simple enough because it was merely a bargain between them in which they would both get something they wanted. Now it wasn't simple at all. She had fallen in love with him, and that was what made the difference.

"Dan," she said simply, "I wish I could make you understand one thing. I love you. If you want to be a cowhand, then that's what I want you to be."

"It won't do," he said.

"Are you trying to tell me you aren't going to marry me?"

He lowered his gaze. "I'm just telling you that neither of us would be happy."

She fought down the rising tide of panic. "Let's not talk about it any more." Taking his arm, she led him back to the love seat. "I haven't said so, but I think it was wonderful the way you brought the bank's money back. Tell me about the fight with the outlaws."

He told her, sitting stiffly beside her. When he finished, she asked, "Hap was the young one, wasn't he?"

"That's right."

"And when I kissed you, he said he wished I was mad at him. Or something like that. He's sweet. I'm glad he got away."

"So am I." Reardon looked at his watch. "I've got to go. It's almost time for Collie's funeral."

"I'll go with you, Dan. I liked Collie, too. Wait till I get my coat."

Astha ran into the dining-room. "Dad, I'm going with Dan to Collie's funeral. We'll take your buggy."

Quinn had started eating. He looked up from his plate, frowning helplessly as he did when she plunged into something he didn't like. He grunted, "All right."

A moment later she was back in the library. "I'm ready, Dan."

They walked across the lawn, the grass beginning to brown from the first fall frosts. She could not tell, looking sideways at him, whether he would rather have gone alone or not.

Later they stood beside the grave and listened to the preacher. It was a short service, and Astha realized that most of those who were there had come from curiosity, morbid people who found a strange pleasure in attending funerals. Only Dan had been Collie Knapp's close friend; only Dan felt the keen edge of sorrow at his death.

When it was over, they walked across the cemetery to the buggy. They were close to the stamp mill here, its throbbing rumble jarring Astha's nerves. Again she felt that quick upsurge of panic and fought it down. Until last spring she had thought she was perfectly happy, that Pat Quinn's power and wealth were enough to satisfy every desire that was in her. Now her existence seemed trivial, worthless. Dan Reardon came from another world, a grim world that was Spartan in its simplicity. More than that— and it was this which gave him his fascination for her—

he was driven by motives which she had never known before and did not understand.

She touched his arm. "I'm sorry about Collie, Dan. I know how much you thought of him."

He looked across the river to the great peaks, bold granite points lifting sharply toward a cerulean sky. "I thought of taking him back to the valley to be buried, but I think he'd like it better here." He looked down at her, stirred by his memories. "He wanted to die like a man, and this was where he did."

They drove back slowly, Astha sensing his need for silence. When they reached the house, Quinn was waiting. Reardon helped Astha down, and Quinn climbed in. He looked sharply at Reardon, saying, "She's always wrapped me around her finger and she always will. I'll give her anything she wants. Damn it, she knew I would all the time."

Reardon said nothing until Quinn had driven away. Then, looking after the banker as his buggy curved down the steep slope, he said, "He's a crook, and you'll never change him."

"Yes I will, and you'll change me." She bit her lip, adding, "I've been a crook, too. I'll be honest with you."

Reardon shook his head. "No, you'll never change him. Collie was the smartest man I ever knew. He understood himself, but he couldn't change. I don't think we can change. Any of us."

"Yes we can, Dan. You'll see."

"Collie told me not to marry you. He said that some night I'd wake up in bed with you beside me, and I'd hate you. I guess you'd hate me, too."

The panic rushed through her again. She had had many men; there were more she could have had, but this one man she wanted was always just out of her reach. She would have to fight the ghost of Collie Knapp, and that was something she did not know how to do. She could only breathe, "He was wrong, Dan. I'll never hate you and I'll never do anything to make you hate me."

"You haven't been exactly fair. You never told me you'd been married."

She clenched her fists. She couldn't tell him how it had been, that she'd been young and she'd wanted the wrong thing. She couldn't tell him why her father had asked her to marry Mark Sands, and how, later, Quinn had insisted she let other men make love to her because that was the one way they could be brought around to Pat Quinn's side. Nor could she tell him how Mark Sands had started drinking because of her and had provoked a quarrel with a man he didn't know and been killed.

Because she could make no case for herself, she said, "I hoped you'd never hear about that, Dan. It doesn't make any difference now. It's all past."

"It makes a difference to me," he said harshly. "And there's another thing that makes a lot of difference. I love Sue."

She put her hands on his shoulders, a quick involuntary motion, and stood so close to him that he would feel the pressure of her breasts, would smell the fragrance of her hair. She said fiercely, "I'll make you forget her, Dan. Remember how it was? You never went back on a bargain; and I went with the deal. Remember?"

He stepped away from her, his dark face suddenly

grim. "All right, Astha, but I've got a chore to do first. Link Bellew is still alive."

He stepped into the saddle and rode away. Then the panic would not be beaten down. She was crying in a way she had not cried since she was a child.

She ran into the house and up the stairs to her room. She had never thought she would let a man do this to her, never thought that she would become a beggar, wanting a caress, waiting to hear a sweet word honestly given.

There was one way she could have made him think of her as she wanted to, one way she could have made him think of her as a sincere woman who loved him enough to give honestly from her heart. She could have said, "If you love Sue and will be happy with her, I won't hold you to your promise." But that was the one thing she could not bring herself to do. She wanted him and she would have him, even knowing that he loved Sue Lane.

❧ CHAPTER 21 ❧

REARDON stopped at the funeral parlor after he left Astha and paid for Collie Knapp's burial. He walked out quickly, resenting the professional sympathy that the somber-faced undertaker started to give him. Leaving his horse at the stable, he had dinner, then asked at the Conner House about the Lanes.

"They left this morning," the clerk said. "Went back home, I think."

"Thanks," Reardon said, and turned into the street.

For a time he stood under the wooden awning of the Conner House, smoking, eyes on the crowd. He could not be sure in his mind that Link Bellew had left town as Lane had said. Bellew would know that Reardon would never forget him, that as long as they were both in the country, there would be no peace for him.

So it would be settled permanently in the fashion that the country demanded, but Bellew would pick his time and place so that the advantage would be his. Reardon rolled another cigarette and smoked it down, thinking of a dozen places in town where Link Bellew could hide. If he was still in Gold Cup, he would be hiding. Reardon was sure of that, but it was impossible to search all the holes into which Bellew could have crawled.

Reardon looked ahead and he did not like what he saw. There were too many things yet to be done to waste his time playing hide-and-seek with Link Bellew. He might, if Pat Quinn had told it straight about Lane's trail herd, leave the country and keep on running. On the other hand, his hatred might overbalance his cupidity and hold him in Gold Cup until he had finished with Reardon. Or it could bring him to a stop beside the trail, Winchester in his hand.

Just as there would be no peace for Bellew as long as Reardon was alive, so the opposite was true. There could be no peace for Reardon as long as Bellew lived and stayed in the country. Every day would be like this, waiting for a bullet from the rim, a clump of scrub oak, the boulder-strewn side of a dry wash.

Regardless of what lay ahead, there was no reason for Reardon to remain longer in Gold Cup. There was work to do on the Rafter R. He knew, too, that no matter how Ash Lane felt about him, or whether he married Astha, he would be drawn into Broken Bell's troubles. He owed that much to Sue, and he had invested in the outfit.

Reardon threw his cigarette stub into the street and threaded his way through the traffic to the stable. He stepped through the archway, blinking in the gloom, heard the hostler's cry, "Look out!" and plunged sideways. Instinctively he fell flat and rolled, cursing himself for not thinking of this. Bellew must have been watching, had seen him take his buckskin back to the stable, and had come here to wait, knowing that he must return for his horse.

A gun winked brightly in the thin light, the roar of it filling the stable. Reardon had his Colt in his hand then. He was out of the archway, the wall to his back. The first slug had missed, spewing stable litter into his face. Again the ambusher fired, but in his anxiety he hurried his shot, and it was high. Another slug came in, searching for him. Then Reardon saw the dry-gulcher in the fourth stall. Just a part of his head and his arm and the gun. Reardon squeezed off a shot, lunged sideways, and waited. The man was gone from sight.

Horses, spooked by the firing, kicked frantically in their stalls. There was the pound of men's boots on the plank walk outside. The marshal bawled, "What is it this time?"

Reardon came slowly to his feet. "I think it was Bellew. He tried to 'gulch me."

Lacey swore. "I might have known it would be you. Why in hell don't you get out of town?"

"I was starting."

The hostler came along the runway, talking to the

horses. Lacey called, "What happened, Mick?"

"Reardon got in one good shot. That's all. This hombre lost one eye and his brains."

"I asked you what happened."

"I told you," the hostler said irritably. "I've had this tough on my neck ever since Reardon brought his horse in. He figgered Reardon would be back, so he waited. I couldn't do anything. He had me laying on my belly in that stall yonder, and he said he'd drill me the first move I made."

"You did plenty," Reardon said. "If you hadn't hollered, I'd have got it where it would've hurt."

The hostler shifted uncomfortably, eyeing the marshal. He blurted, "This camp owes you something for what you done, even if there's some that don't know it. I couldn't just let that Price hombre drill you."

"Price!" Reardon exclaimed, and strode back along the runway. The dead man was George Price, the Broken Bell rider who had tried to burn his cabin last spring.

The marshal had followed Reardon. He said, "How did this hombre get into the ruckus?"

"He's Bellew's man." Reardon gave the lawman a straight look. "You've got your own notions about me, Lacey. Likewise you've got some queer notions about what murder is. Now what are your intentions?"

"Murder, hell," the hostler broke in. "I saw it, Lacey. You can't hold a man for murder when some ornery son like Price tries to 'gulch him."

The marshal looked at the dead man, then at Reardon. He said with grudging respect, "You're sure hell with that iron, friend."

"If Bellew had plugged me in a fair fight," Reardon said, "nobody would call it murder, but you might as well have let a kid shoot it out with Bellew as Collie Knapp. I still say it's murder."

"You can say whatever you damned please," Lacey said angrily. "Knapp committed suicide. That's all."

Reardon knew that it was true. Lacey could not have stopped it, but Collie was as dead as if Ash Lane had had his way with him in the spring. Reardon had averted the hanging; he had not been able to keep Collie from drawing on Bellew. Collie had not wanted him to. That was the answer. The marshal was more right than he knew when he said Collie had committed suicide.

"All right," Reardon said. "What about this?"

The lawman threw a quick glance at the scowling hostler and on around the circle of men who had fanned out along the runway. They all knew, and their expressions showed it, that Reardon had done the community a favor by returning the bank money. A man less sensitive to public opinion than Lacey could not have mistaken their sentiments.

"It ain't murder in my book when a man kills a back-shooting son like that," he said sourly, "but you've sure turned this camp inside out since you got here. Now dust."

"Friend," Reardon said, "if I never see your lousy burg again, it will be too soon."

Reardon's thoughts were bitterly disturbing as he rode downstream. Ash Lane had said, "Nothing's changed." Lane had a talent for being wrong. Actually, everything was changed. It seemed years ago that Dan Reardon had been riding down the steep south wall of Long Tom

Valley and had let out an exuberant whoop because he felt so good.

He remembered telling Astha that nothing was ever settled. Collie Knapp was dead. George Price was dead. Still nothing was settled. Old wounds into which the salt of deep hatred had been poured would be hard to heal. Or if they did, the scars would remain. It was the ancient pattern of hate begetting hate.

Reardon thought of Astha then. He had never seen her before as she had been today. Desperate. Frantic. Uncertain of herself, yet somehow forcing her father back into line. Holding Reardon to his promise. Clutching with grim tenacity the thing which she wanted. Or did she really want him?

He was not sure, even now, whether Astha had been entirely honest today. He thought of Sue, impatient, hasty, impetuous, plunging ahead without seeing where she was going. Caution was not in her. Perhaps it never would be. Life with her would be as exciting and full of surprises as a ride on a wild horse, but whatever her failings were, dishonesty was not one of them. But Astha was entirely different. That was the proof of what Knapp had said, that some day he'd hate her if he married her. He could never fully trust her.

Today he had gone to the Quinn house resolved to hold himself away from Astha, to break everything off. Well, he hadn't. She had refused to let him go. She had kissed him, and in spite of all his intentions, he had been shaken by the sweetness of her lips.

It was dusk when Reardon found the Lanes camped along the river. He reined up waiting for Ash to say, "Get down," but the old man only stared truculently at him, keeping the wall high between them. It was Sue who said, "Light and rest your saddle, Dan. I thought you'd be along, so I saved supper for you."

Reardon watered his horse and returned to the Lane campfire. He ate in silence, the pressure of Ash Lane's eyes stirring resentment in him. When he finished his coffee, he set his tin cup down. He said, "I killed George Price this afternoon."

"Why?" Sue asked.

He told them how it had been, adding, "Looks to me, Ash, like Link assays pretty low-grade. George had the guts to make a try, but Link was somewhere else."

"George had reason," Lane said in a ragged voice. "He never forgot that walk you took him on last spring."

Reardon opened his mouth, then closed it, saying nothing. There was no use arguing with the old man. Ash Lane was something else that would never change. He sat hunkered by the fire like a great brooding eagle. Reardon thought, *He knows he's wrong, but he'd shoot himself before he'd say so.*

Then, for the first time, Reardon felt some sympathy for Lane. Quinn had surrendered to Astha, thereby admitting his love for her and admitting that his only happiness, aside from his satisfaction in building a fortune, stemmed from his daughter's happiness. Lane was not capable of such a surrender. Whatever happened now, Lane and Sue would never feel the same toward each other as they had six months ago.

Reardon rose, knowing he could not stay here. He said quite casually, "Thanks, Sue. I was getting a little lank."

Sue forced a smile. "I thought you would be."

He stood looking at her in the firelight, his throat tightening. The last months had changed this small, proud girl as tempering heat would change a steel blade. She had curbed her impatience. She held herself completely under control, smiling a little, wanting him and letting him see it, yet making no cheapening move toward him.

He said, "I'll be sloping along." He walked to his buckskin and stepped into the saddle.

Sue followed him to his horse. Then, with the reins in his hands, she said, "We're broke. Dad will die swearing he's right about Bellew. I understand now how my mother had to live." She made a small gesture as if she was very tired. "I don't suppose I'll be in the valley much longer. Good luck if I don't see you again."

"Ash will pull something out. He's got a year before he has to pay Quinn anything again."

"Good-by, Dan."

He said, "Good-by," lifted his hat, and rode away.

❧ CHAPTER 22 ❧

REARDON did not go to his cabin when he returned to the valley. Instead of crossing the river, he turned his horse up the steep trail to Garnet Mesa. Cold weather had started his cows toward the lower country, so he did not have to ride as far into the jumble of gulches and canyons as he had thought he would.

There was, he found, some loss, but it was less than he had any right to expect. He gathered the she stuff, calves and yearlings, and after three days of riding, had them off the mesa and into the valley. He turned them into the brush along the river where they would find good graze for a time. Meanwhile he would have to rustle some hay, and the money he had left was hardly enough.

Dusk was flowing across the valley in darkening purple waves when Reardon rode across the bridge and reined up in front of Jess Vance's store. Talley's horse, he saw, was anchored to the hitchrack.

Reardon walked into the store, glad that the last three days were behind him. He had been alone too long with his thoughts, too long with the knowledge that he still had some chores to do and he wasn't sure how he could do them. He had told himself time after time that whatever happened to Broken Bell and Broken Bell's trail herd was up to Ash Lane. He had done what he had for Lane largely because of Sue and because he did not want Lane to be destroyed, but now the last of a small sympathy for Lane was gone. He was intent upon destroying himself, and Reardon would do no more, even for Sue. But Bellew was still the problem.

Talley was standing at the bar, a half-empty whisky bottle in front of him. He swung around when he heard Reardon's heels on the floor and raised a hand in greeting. "Howdy, Dan. Just where in hell have you been?"

"Fetching my stuff down off Garnet Mesa." Reardon came up to the bar. "Left 'em on the other side of the river. Ash will raise Cain when he hears, figgering that piece of grass is his like he figgers everything else is his. So I guess having an interest in Broken Bell won't keep me from fighting Ash."

Talley had started to pour another drink. He put the

bottle back on the bar. "Now say that last over, slow like."

Reardon laughed and reached for the bottle. "I need that worse than you do. Where's Jess?"

"In back." Talley got another glass and set it in front of Reardon. "I want to know about that interest in Broken Bell. Sounds to me like you're drunk."

"Damned good idea." Reardon took his drink. Then he told Talley about his break with Quinn and about paying Lane's debt. "That's the way it stands, Hap. The whole thing started over Collie. I figgered that with him gone, Ash might be different, but, hell, I should have known better."

Talley stood turning his empty glass, staring down at it. He showed none of the resentment that had been in him the night of the fight at Gebhardt's, but something, Reardon saw, was troubling him.

Finally Talley cuffed back his hat with a thumb. He said, "I've got the U.P. dinero. I'm sending it back. All of it. I've figgered some on what you said." He poured a drink and let it stand. "Reckon you're right. Guess I knew it all the time, but it's took all that's happened to make me see it."

"That's fine, Hap," Reardon said. "'Bout the only good news I've had lately."

Talley pinned his gaze on Reardon's face and blurted, "I'd be smart to ride a thousand miles from here, but damn it, I kind of like this country. I've been thinking that mebbe you could use a hand. I know that with a record like I have—"

"Hold on," Reardon broke in. "There's nobody I'd rather have riding for me than you, but I ain't got nothing but a shirttail outfit, and I don't know when I'll have anything better. I can't even pay you wages."

"Then you'll take me on, knowing what you do—"

"Sure, if you want to work for beans." Reardon grinned. "Looks like that's what I'll be eating all winter."

"It's a deal. Beans sure stay with a man."

"I don't reckon we're out of the woods." Reardon told him about the fight with George Price. "I've got to go after Bellew. Should have come right on, I reckon, but I kept thinking about my stuff on the mesa. They ought to have been down before this." He took a drink and wiped his mouth with his sleeve. "If Bellew's got Ash's herd over the pass, I don't look for him to show up here no more. The proposition is that I ain't sure if I ought to go after him or not. Collie used to say that hate could burn a man out quicker'n anything else. Mebbe I ought to forget him."

"You'll have a hell of a time forgetting him," Talley said. "He's got the Broken Bell herd at the foot of the pass."

Reardon stiffened. "Then he's aiming to double-cross Quinn. He'll give Ash some cock-and-bull yarn about why he didn't have the cattle at Placerville, and Ash'll believe it."

Jess Vance had come out of the back room in time to hear what Reardon said. He walked along the bar, the deep lines in his face mute evidence of the worry that had long been in them. "Dan, you started this trouble last spring. Now it's rolling like a snowball down a mountain. Where's it going to stop?"

Angry, Reardon said, "You're hell on blaming the other gent, Jess. You were here in the valley a long time before I was. Why didn't you whittle Ash down?"

Vance waved Reardon's words aside. "We'd been getting along. But I didn't mean that. I'm talking about you bringing Quinn into the deal. He said you and him had split up, which I knew you would sooner or later. He's a bigger crook than Ash—"

"When did you see Quinn?" Reardon broke in.

Vance turned to Talley. "Didn't you tell him?"

"No." Talley frowned. "I was getting around to it."

"The Quinns got here this afternoon," Vance said. "Burned the breeze from Gold Cup the way the horses looked. When Quinn found out Bellew still had the trail herd in the valley, he was ready to climb the wall. Never seen a madder man."

"Where is he?"

"He lit out for Bellew's camp. I fed 'em. Astha was about ready to fall over, so I gave her my bed. She's sleeping now. She asked about you, and when I said you hadn't showed up, she got almighty worried. Maybe I oughtta wake her up—"

"No. Sue and Ash back yet?"

"Sue is. She went home. She said Ash caved when he didn't find the herd at Placerville like he figgered he would. He stayed at Houston's ranch, and Sue rode on home to see what happened to the herd."

"Keep Astha here, Jess." Reardon jerked his head at Talley. "Let's ride, Hap."

"What am I supposed to tell Astha?" Vance shouted. "She looked like she was gonna keel over when I said you hadn't showed. I used to think she was hoorawing you 'bout being in love with you, but she wasn't play-acting today."

"Tell her I'll be back," Reardon said, and left the store, Talley following.

When they were in their saddles, Talley asked, "Just what are we heading into?"

"Trouble. While ago I was wondering whether I ought to forget Bellew. I ain't wondering now. If I've made any mistake this summer, it was not killing him when I had a chance."

They left the store, riding westward. A few minutes later they passed Reardon's cabin, a small, low shadow in the gathering darkness.

"I've seen you work," Talley said. "Just offhand I'd say you're the best man with a six I ever met up with, but looks to me like you're pushing your luck too far on this deal."

"Why?"

"Bellew's got his boys in camp. There's only about three of the old hands that you used to work with according to Vance. Now if you go helling into camp, we'll be swapping lead with the whole bunch. There's just too damned many of 'em."

Reardon rode in silence for a moment, thinking about it. Finally he said, "This is a job of snake stomping. Somebody's got to do it, and the sooner it's done, the better. I figger Quinn half believed Ash when Ash told him Bellew took his money but didn't aim to steal the herd so he's here to find out. Mebbe Quinn'll get what's coming to him, and I ain't gonna worry 'bout him, but long as Bellew's in the country, there'll be trouble of some kind."

"Don't look like he aims to steal Lane's cattle," Talley said thoughtfully, "or he'd have started 'em afore this.

There'll be snow in the pass any time now."

Again Reardon was silent, a new thought driving a chill of fear down his spine. Then he said, "Hap, I'm guessing, but it makes sense. Bellew's wanted Sue all the time. Now suppose he did aim to run that herd into Utah. What would he do to make sure Ash wouldn't send an outfit after him?"

"He might be waiting for Sue to get back so he could nab her, but that'd be more'n crazy. Stealing a girl is a hell of a lot worse than stealing cows."

"Depends. He could leave word that he'd drop Sue off at Moab, but if there was any pursuit, Ash would never see her again."

Reardon sleeved sweat from his forehead. It was crazy, but Bellew was not a rational man. He had made love to Sue, and she had refused to have anything to do with him. He was capable of striking back regardless of the hornets' nest it would stir up.

"He's in over his neck all right," Talley agreed. "You might be calling it right."

It was almost completely dark now with just a haze of light lingering above the western rim. The faint drum of horses sounded ahead, and Reardon, hearing it first, reined up. Talley stopped, and they sat their saddles for a time, listening.

"Not many," Talley murmured. "Three or four, I'd say, and they're heading this way."

"We'll wait," Reardon said, and pulled off the road into the tall sagebrush.

They came a few minutes later, traveling slowly. Three men, Reardon saw, and drew his gun. When they were almost abreast, he called, "Hook the moon, boys."

They stopped and raised their hands. One asked, "That you, Reardon?"

It was Ben Freed, one of the old hands who had been with Broken Bell long before Bellew had come to the valley. Reardon rode out of the sagebrush, saying, "Yeah. Who's with you?"

"Chuck and Slim."

These were the three who would not follow Link Bellew. Reardon holstered his gun. "What's going on, Ben?"

"Hell," Freed said bitterly. "I never did cotton to Bellew like Ash did. Now I know why. He'd make a snake look plumb honest."

"What happened?" Reardon pressed.

"He killed Quinn for one thing. Not that I figger it's any loss, but Quinn ain't no gun hand."

"Damn it," Reardon shouted. "Are you gonna tell me what happened?"

"Well, we've been sitting around when that herd should have been on the trail more'n a week ago. Bellew was gone part of that time. Dunno where, but after we made the gather, he said to hold 'em yonder at the foot of the pass. When he got back, he said to keep on holding 'em. Never said why. He was gone when Quinn drove his buggy into camp. Quinn cussed plenty and wanted to know why the herd was still here. Seems like he had a fool notion we was gonna push 'em into Utah. 'Bout dusk Bellew rode in, and Quinn started cussing him. Claimed Bellew double-crossed him. Bellew stood there taking the worst rawhiding I ever heard a man take. Purty soon he blew up, poked Quinn in the snoot, and knocked him into the fire. Quinn yelped and made a grab for his gun. Bellew plugged him in the belly."

"Why are you boys heading this way?"

"Bellew gave us our time and said we was done. Told us to get out of the valley." Freed swore bitterly. "I've got all stove up riding for this outfit and I'm too old to start hunting for another job. I'm gonna see Ash afore I pull out. I don't figger he'll stand for this. Why, hell—"

"I don't reckon Ash will stand for it, Ben," Reardon broke in. "Bellew aims to steal that herd. What did he do after you got your time?"

"Dunno. We lit a shuck out of there, but we hadn't gone more'n a hundred yards till we heard a horse heading out of camp on the run."

"Going where?"

"Too dark to see good, but he was starting toward Broken Bell."

'The fear became a knot in Reardon's middle. He said in a tight voice, "Talley, you and these boys head for camp. They'll move the herd over the pass in the morning if I'm guessing right. You'd best stampede 'em. Scatter 'em to hellangone. If Bellew is up to what I think he is, he won't take time to gather 'em again."

"I dunno 'bout this," Freed said dubiously. "You ain't been on Lane's side. How do we know—"

"You don't," Reardon said, "but you'd better believe I don't aim to let Bellew have them cows. I'll get somebody to take Quinn's body into camp. Then I'm going after Bellew. I figger I know where to look."

CHAPTER 23

I T was late afternoon when Sue Lane reached Broken Bell and turned her horse into the pasture. The place appeared to be deserted, and that was strange until she remembered that the cook was probably in camp. She walked through the house, finding no one, and built a fire in the kitchen stove. She stood beside it, listening to the wood crackle and holding her hands out to it, for the house was cold. There had been, she thought, no fire in the stove for several days.

She cooked supper, and by the time she had eaten, darkness had moved across the valley. She ate without conscious thought, the memory of her father's face haunting her. He had never, as long as she could remember, admitted he was wrong about anything. Nor had he admitted it when they had reached Placerville and found that the herd was not there. They had talked to a man who had just come up the canyon. There was, he said, no herd bedded down along the river.

For a long time Ash Lane had sat in the hotel lobby staring at the wall, faded blue eyes almost closed, motionless except for the steady brushing of his mustache.

"Let's go to bed," Sue said.

"No."

He had kept on brushing his mustache as if he had turned a machine on and had forgotten to turn it off. He knew at last, Sue thought, that Link Bellew had sold him out. Through all the hours since they had left Gold Cup he had been kept going by his unswerving faith in his judgment of men.

Watching him, Sue had thought for a moment that he was dying. His eyes were glassy, his face gray and drawn. Finally he brought himself stiffly to his feet. He said, "All right. We'll go to bed."

He had ridden all the next day in his buggy, Sue beside him on her horse, and he'd said nothing until they had reached Houston's ranch. Then he said, "Reckon I'd better stay here tomorrow," and he'd tumbled out of the buggy in a dead faint. He had come out of it and been able to eat supper. The next morning she had promised him she'd find out about the herd, and had ridden on by herself.

She washed the dishes and put them away, thinking she should saddle up and ride to camp, but she was too tired. Besides, Vance had told her the herd was being held at the base of the pass. If Bellew had not stolen it with all the time he'd had, it was unlikely he'd steal it now. She'd go in the morning.

Carrying the lamp into the front room, she set it on the table and went onto the front porch. For a few minutes she stood staring at the sky and the long black rim to the south. The drum of running horses came to her, and she wondered about it. Suddenly she stiffened, the wind bringing a faint whisper of sound. From the bunkhouse, she thought, an involuntary shiver chilling her. She had often been here alone and she had never been afraid, but tonight danger seemed to be pressed in all around her. There was silence again, and the chill of fear passed.

For no reason that she was aware of, she thought of Dan Reardon, no reason except that he was seldom out of her mind. It would always be that way, she knew. The bitterness she had once felt toward him was entirely gone, for she understood a great deal that she had not understood six months before.

Ash Lane was a relic of a past generation. There had been many like him in the cattle business; there would be few in the future, for men of Dan Reardon's caliber would take the reins out of their hands as law moved in on the open range. It was still a world of dust and brute force and violence, and Dan fitted into it, but there was a quality in him that her father had never known. Perhaps a sense of responsibility, the knowledge that there were other demands to which a man must answer besides his own driving ambition.

Broken Bell would never be the same as it had been through her growing years. Collie Knapp! Pat Quinn! Link Bellew! These men had had a part of what had happened this summer, but she saw clearly that their roles were the minor ones, filling in the details of incident. In reality the conflict had been between her father and Dan. They were the opposite poles. It had been strength against strength, will against will, one kind of faith against another. She thought she knew what the end would be. Ash Lane would be gone, and Dan Reardon would remain, and everything in the valley would be different. It was the change of the tide.

She shivered again, not certain whether it was the evening chill, or whether a trace of fear was still in her. Turning, she went inside, wishing she could lock the house, but locks were unknown to Ash Lane. It was part of the massive self-confidence which was so much a part of him. She climbed the stairs, shut the door, and set the lamp on her bureau.

Pulling out a drawer, she took out a small revolver and laid it beside the lamp. It was foolish, for all of the violence that had touched the valley had been between men. Women were safe. Still, she could not shake off the feeling that someone was around.

It was then a few minutes after nine. She moved to the window, but she could see nothing. Again the sound of running horses came to her. More to the west now, close to the foot of the pass. Then a sudden burst of gunfire. She did not know what it was about. Bellew would not be moving the herd tonight. There was little she could do if he started them over the La Sals in the morning. She was one woman against half a dozen men who belonged to Link Bellew. There were three others she could depend upon, but without leadership, they would be of little value.

She turned away from the bureau and started unbuttoning her shirt. Then she stopped, fingers paralyzed. She heard the creak of a board on the stairs, a man's low curse. It was Link Bellew's voice.

For what seemed an eternity Sue could not move. There was no sound but the quick sharp pant of her breathing. Her heart was hammering as if it would break loose from her chest. Then she came alive, darted to the bureau, and picked up her gun. She heard the door open and swung toward it. Bellew stood there, grinning, the corners of his mouth brown with tobacco stain, yellow eyes alive with desire. She fired point-blank and missed.

That was her one chance. He was on her with catlike

speed. Her second shot was wild, slapping into the wall beside the door. Then he had her right wrist and twisted until she dropped the gun. Crying out, she beat at him with her left hand, kicked his shin, bit him, but his arms were steel bands. He picked her up and held her hard against him, laughing in her face, the smell of his breath the nauseating stink of chewed tobacco.

"I told you a long time ago that I never seen a filly I couldn't tame," he said. "You didn't believe me, but now you'll see."

He kissed her. She must have fainted, for there was a moment that afterward held no memory for her. He blew out the lamp and, carrying her in his arms, started down the dark stairs. She had been limp. Now she stiffened, jerked a hand free, and rammed a thumb into his eye. He let out a squall of pain, slipped, and fell, and they went down the stairs, smashing into the wall and finally slamming against the floor at the bottom.

They both lay there for a moment, breath beaten out of them. Sue regained hers first and started to crawl away. He saw her in the starlight washing in through a window, grabbed her by an ankle and jerked her flat. Pulling her back toward him, he held her against him, his mouth close to her face.

"Look, Sue. I don't want to hurt you. I'm taking the trail herd in the morning, and you're my insurance against Ash sending a bunch after us. Now behave."

"I'll kill you," she screamed.

She rammed her face against his, opened her mouth, and bit his nose. He yelled again in pain and slapped her loose. He cursed, shouting, "Damn it, I told you I didn't want to hurt you. I've waited a long time for this."

He got to his feet and jerked her upright, gripping her so hard she could not breathe. She kicked him, and he hit her again. She went slack in his arms, almost unconscious, only faintly aware that the front door was swinging open. She must be dreaming, for she heard Dan Reardon say, "All right, Link. Get away from her."

Bellew dropped her and clawed for his gun. Reardon fired, a bright ribbon lancing the darkness. Sue heard Bellew cry out, saw flame spurt from his gun. She grabbed at his leg and tugged, wanting to do something.

Reardon shouted, "Get out of the way, Sue," and she rolled clear.

More firing, a wild chaotic scene that engulfed her with its violence, noise racketing against her ears, powdersmoke smell that was stifling, points of dancing gunfire. Then it was over, and stillness pressed against her, strange, unreal.

She wanted to scream, to ask Dan if he was all right, but no sound came from her dry, aching throat. Then she heard a body crash to the floor, and Dan asked, "Where are you, Sue?"

She came to her feet. She answered in a strange voice she did not know. "Here, Dan."

"Stay where you are," Reardon said.

She heard him cross the room, the crack of his spike heels on the floor, glimpsed the shadowy passage of his tall body. A match flame splashed into the darkness and went out.

Reardon said, "It's finished."

She sucked in a long ragged breath until her lungs

almost burst, and stumbled across the room to him. She put her hands on his arms, on his shoulders, felt of his face, and then she began to cry. She was shaking, her knees were water, and he held her that way for a long time and let her cry.

❧ CHAPTER 24 ❧

IT was early morning when Hap Talley rode into Broken Bell's yard and called. Reardon came out of the barn, asking, "How did it go?"

Talley grinned and raised a hand to a bloody bandage around his head. "Fine as silk, Dan. I got this, and Freed got tagged in his left arm. That's all the souvenirs we got, and we scattered them steers from hell to breakfast. Where's Bellew?"

Reardon told him. Talley nodded. "I kind of figgered it would be that way." He scratched his nose, hesitated, and then said, "Jess got one of the settlers to haul Quinn's body to Gold Cup, and Astha wants me to drive her back. Any kick?"

"Hell, no."

"She's your girl, ain't she?"

Reardon lowered his head and busied himself with a cigarette. This was another fork in the trail. He sealed the cigarette and slit it into his mouth, raising his eyes to Talley.

"I don't know, Hap. I've got to talk to her, but either way, I'd like it if you'd see she gets back to Gold Cup."

"She's at the store waiting for you."

Reardon swung toward the corral, calling over his

shoulder, "Better stay here till I get back. I don't like to leave Sue alone."

Astha was standing beside the stove in the back of the store when Reardon racked his buckskin and went in. He closed the door against the frosty morning air and stood against it, eyes on the girl. She stood tall and very straight, her face composed. Somehow she had steeled herself against any show of grief, but Reardon knew how it had been with her and her father. She would miss him more in another month than she did now.

Vance was puttering with something behind the counter. Without a word he went out. Reardon heard the clatter of a rig on the bridge, swung to the window, and saw Ash Lane drive past. When he turned back, Astha had moved to the front of the store and stood a step from him.

He said hesitantly, fumbling for the right words, "I'm sorry about Pat. I know how—"

"Don't be sorry for him, Dan," she said quietly. "He had more than anyone else on the western slope, but it wasn't enough. If Bellew hadn't done it, someone else would. The only wonder is that it hadn't been done before. If there is anything I have learned since I've met you, it's that you can't go on smashing other people without having it kick back into your own face sooner or later."

"Pat was what he was," Reardon said. "I told you none of us could change."

"I have," she said. "If there has been anything good come out of all this, I guess that's it. If I had been any other woman in Gold Cup, I'd have been called a tramp or worse, but being Astha Quinn, my morals were my own business. The way Dad saw it and the way he raised me, infidelity was no sin, but being so honest that it hurt was more than a sin; it was crazy."

Now, for the first time since he had known her, he sensed that she was being brutally honest with him.

"It's justice of a sort, I suppose," she hurried on. "Dad brought about his own death, and I've lived so that you don't want me. I don't blame you and I won't try to make you marry me. I've offered myself and more money than you'd make out of a million cows, but it isn't enough. So," she held out her hand, "it's good-by. I saw things different after I heard Dad had been killed. Trying to make you keep a bargain that was a mistake in the first place would be Dad's way. It's no good, Dan."

He took her hand and held it, eyes searching her face. It told him nothing. He said, "Good-by. If you ever want—"

"We'll chop it off, Dan. Clean."

After he left the store she moved to the window and watched him mount and ride away, sitting his saddle easily as a man born to it. She breathed, "It's like Dad said. He'll be a cowhand all his life, and nobody could ever change him."

Vance was there beside her, eyes on Reardon until he disappeared toward Broken Bell. He said, "There goes a man. He's grown ten feet tall since last spring."

"A man," she breathed, "and the best thing that ever happened to me."

Talley was waiting in front of Lane's house when Reardon rode back into Broken Bell's yard. He said somberly, "I just heard Sue tell Ash what happened last night, Dan. You should have killed that damned stinking Bellew slow like, fixed it so it took him a week to die."

"I reckon," Reardon said. "You can slope along. I think Astha's ready."

Talley lifted his reins. "I'll be back. Don't go off chasing rainbows."

"No rainbows in this country. If I chase anything, it'll be a cow."

Talley grinned and rode away. Reardon stepped down and racked his horse. Sue was not in sight, but Ash Lane sat on his rocking chair, his bad leg propped up on the porch railing.

Reardon said, "Howdy," and was shocked by the old man's appearance. His cheeks were sunken, the skin of his face ghastly gray. The years had caught up with him in less than a week.

"Howdy," Ash said. "Glad you're here. Wanted to talk to you." He shifted in his rocker and stared eastward down the long trough of the valley as if trying to picture again the way things had been. "I'm lighting out for Ouray and see what them hot springs can do for me. No sense fooling myself. I'm in bad shape. Ain't got much cash, but when you get back from Denver after selling my trail herd, I'll have enough to pay for my bacon and beans, and you'll have enough to run Broken Bell."

Hot words were on Reardon's tongue. This was like Lane, taking everything for granted. He said, "What the hell, Ash. I've got Rafter R—"

"You get hold of Freed and the other boys," Lane went on as if he hadn't heard. "Pick up some of the neighbors and gather them steers. Talley told me what happened. Get 'em on the trail. You'll find cars waiting on the narrow gauge at Placerville." He shifted in his chair again, biting his lips against the pain that racked him. "You'll have a good outfit here, Dan. You and Sue."

Then the anger died in Reardon. This was Lane's way of telling him he'd made one kind of a mistake in Bellew, another in him, and he was surrendering. He had never bent his pride more than he was doing now; he could not bend it enough to say that he'd been wrong. This was what Reardon wanted. It was the end of the bowing and scraping to Ash Lane.

"I'll get right at it, Ash," Dan said.

Lane motioned toward the house. "She's in the kitchen." He stared at the south rim, the red sandstone sharply lighted by the morning sun. He breathed, "Funny, Dan. Damned funny. That wall looked just the same when I came. It won't be any different a thousand years from now."

Reardon crossed the porch and went back through the house into the kitchen. Sue, hearing him, looked up and smiled and poured her cake dough into a pan. He came to her, saying, "Astha's going back to Gold Cup. She said it was no good keeping a bargain that was a mistake in the first place."

"I'm glad." Sue opened the oven door and slid the pan inside.

"Looks like we're partners," Reardon said.

Turning, she faced him and waited, saying nothing. For a moment he looked at her, thinking of that night in the tamarack brush along the river. Then he put it out of his mind. Time that is behind a man cannot be lived over, but the time that is ahead still belongs to him, and the living of it is in his hands.

"I love you," he said. "There has never been a day since I met you when I didn't. I've had some bad times the last six months. I don't want any more of it away from you."

She moved toward him, holding out the diamond ring she had once thrown at him. "Put it back where it belongs, Dan. I rode to your cabin after you had gone that morning and hunted till I found it. I kept hoping that it would be like this sometime."

He slipped it on her finger, suddenly humbled by what he sensed in her. Then her hands were on his arms and he felt the old impatience in her again. He drew her to him and, tilting her face up to his, tasted the wild, sweet flavor of her lips.

Center Point Publishing
600 Brooks Road • PO Box 1
Thorndike ME 04986-0001 USA

(207) 568-3717

US & Canada:
1 800 929-9108